WINTER CHANCE

Walking in Wolf Tracks  by Ron Gamer

D1502575

Prologue

P R O L O G U E

The young man saw no other choice. Whether he could afford the time or not, he had to take a break. Forward progress came at a huge cost, as he battled a biting wind and deep snow. Every muscle and nerve, every ligament and joint, pleaded for a recess. He huddled up against the paper-like bark of a birch tree—gulping in mouthfuls of air. When breathing slowed, and his pulse stopped pounding, the teen tilted his face skyward.

Apparently Mother Nature hadn't completed her work. Several feet of fresh white powder already carpeted the forest floor. And from the appearance of slate-colored clouds overhead, another round of redecorating was about to begin.

Pushing down panic, the youth lowered his gaze and resumed plodding in the general direction of the trail. If he were to save himself, the narrow forest path had to be reached before dark. He didn't dare linger. That could prove fatal, and he wasn't ready to die.

The teenager was positive the weather gods held a grudge against him. The forecast promised clear skies and more days of above-normal temperatures. Yeah, he brooded, just like the prediction for the autumn adventure. Why hadn't the lesson been learned the first time?

WINTER CHANCE

Walking in Wolf Tracks 🐾 by Ron Gamer

Adventure Publications, Inc.
CAMBRIDGE, MINNESOTA

dedication

For Avary, Davis, Nate, Parker, and Grace—
may your lives be filled with wonder and every
adventure close with a happy ending.

Cover and book design by Jonathan Norberg

Copyright 2003 by Ron Gamer
Published by Adventure Publications, Inc.
820 Cleveland St. S
Cambridge, MN 55008
1-800-678-7006
Printed in the U.S.A.
ISBN: 1-59193-024-3

This two day trip seemed so simple—so safe—and the perfect prescription for a private dilemma. Catch a ride up the Gunflint Trail, then hike to an out-of-the-way wilderness lake. Set up camp, do some winter fishing, and bed down for the night. Trek back to the blacktop around noon the next day. Easy enough. But like so often happens in life, things hadn't gone as planned. Who could have possibly foreseen Old Man Winter joining forces with a pair of ill-tempered outlaws? Working as a team, the trio had managed to transform this innocent outing into a life or death survival test.

Reflecting back, the youngster realized he should have heeded his mother's words. She'd warned him about the dangers of camping out alone. But he hadn't paid much attention. Although it was too late now, he was wishing he'd taken her motherly advice.

Chapter One

C H A P T E R   O N E

Travis Larsen quietly shut the storm door before step-ping out into the crisp air. The lanky teen paused to gaze out over Poplar Lake. A thin slice of watermelon pink glowed softly on the far horizon, holding promise for a sensational sunrise. From all indications another beautiful day was in store for the Boundary Waters Wilderness Area.

He took a moment to check the large round thermometer nestled near the kitchen window and smiled. The over-sized needle pointed to twenty-eight degrees. Not cold for northern Minnesota during the last week of December.

Eager, but a bit nervous, Travis took review of his win-ter gear. An all-weather parka over a pair of bib-styled snowmobile pants made up the outer shell. Closer to his skin he wore long underwear, a turtleneck top, and a thick wool shirt. Tucked inside felt-lined boots, his feet were warm and snug cocooned in two pairs of socks. And completing the wardrobe, atop his long sandy-colored hair, perched a bright blue stocking hat. With an extra pair of gloves, and an insulated vest stowed in the pack, he had more than enough clothing to stay warm.

After snatching up the loaded packframe and clutching it to his chest in a bear hug, Travis bounced down the flight of steps leading to the beach area. His best friend was to meet him at first light. Seth Springwood and his family helped run a resort a half mile down the shore. Only several cabins were winterized. There wasn't much work to be done this time of year. With scant snow cover and weeks of warm weather, the retreat had few paying customers.

All of which meant Seth had plenty of idle time. It was unfortunate his injured ankle wasn't ready for a long hike. He would have enjoyed the trek. Seth loved outdoor adventure—couldn't get enough of it. Like Travis, Seth considered the Boundary Waters Wilderness Area merely an extension of his own backyard—a big place to play.

At the edge of the lake, Travis turned and began trudging along the shoreline. As if walking on egg shells, every step he took caused crusty snow to crunch underfoot, spoiling the quiet stillness of predawn. Coming upon several sections of dock stacked for the winter months, he plunked down and began inspecting the camping gear.

His eyes lingered on snowshoes tied tightly to the rear of the carrier. The wooden frames looked so shiny and new in the soft light. These weren't ordinary store-bought shoes; they were special and he treasured them. Under the shop teacher's critical eye, Travis had hand-crafted the shoes himself. And though he was hoping to put the shoes to good use, they probably wouldn't be needed for this outing. What little snow remained was thin and icy.

Travis finished taking inventory, and then sat quietly, waiting for his ride to arrive. Off to the southeast the sun was planning to make a grand entrance. Muted pinks and reds were being shoved aside. In their place, golden shafts of yellow light burst over the horizon, reminding Travis of sunrises often pictured on the cover of the local church bulletin.

The longer the teen sat huddled on the dock, the brighter the new day became. With light, some of his earlier worry seemed to melt away. Going on an overnight ice-fishing expedition had been his idea. His father had been quick to give the okay. It was his mother who had needed convincing. His dad argued that they had to let their son grow up. Eventually, with enough nagging, his mom relented and gave the go-ahead.

It was Travis himself who had doubts about the overnight outing. Not that he was going far. Only a four or five mile hike to a narrow, off the path, wilderness lake. He hadn't told a soul about his personal problem. And like an unattended blister, the secret had festered and grown—gnawing away at self-confidence. It was time for a cure and only he could play doctor.

Travis was lost in thought and at first didn't notice the whine of the snowmobile in the distance. The machine was rounding the wooded point a few hundred yards farther down the lake. The driver was staying near shore, no doubt concerned about thin ice. Rider and sled cleared the peninsula, and then headed straight for the Larsens', a vapor trail lingering behind in the still morning air.

The drone of the engine grew in volume as the machine approached. When the snowmobile pulled parallel to the shoreline, both it and the noise came to an abrupt halt. With the ease of youth, the driver flipped the helmet visor, flashed a wide smile, and in a husky voice asked, "Been waitin' long?"

"Nope, just got here," Travis replied, pushing up from the dock. "You're right on time."

Pursing lips while tipping his head in thought, the new-comer studied Travis for several seconds. "Trav, you sure that you want to do this? Didn't you get enough sleeping out in October?"

"Yeah, you're just jealous 'cause you can't come along. I know if ya could, you'd be right beside me."

"Yup. Hate to admit it, but you're right," Seth said, grinning. The brawny teenager lifted a leg over the snowmobile seat and stood to stretch. "Why don't you put your stuff in the storage rack? Then you can tell me where we're headed."

Using both hands, Travis lifted his backpack and placed it in the metal framed box attached to the rear of the machine. "Should I use a bungee cord or do you think it'll stay put without one?" he asked, facing his friend.

As if he were a mind reader, Seth had expected the question. A large rubber stretch cord was dangling from his hand. "Here, rookie. I didn't think you'd remember to bring one of these. Hmm...I wonder what else you forgot? Got a lighter so you can make a fire tonight?"

Travis nodded. "And would ya knock off that 'rookie' business. Of course I brought a lighter. It's in my pants pocket. Extra matches, too. And I didn't forget to bring bungees. I have a couple of spares in the pack."

"What about a flashlight?" Seth asked, plopping back down on the seat cushion.

"For sure. Fresh batteries to boot."

"Map? Did you remember a map or are ya just gonna wing it?"

Travis patted one of the pockets of his parka. "Gotta map. Shouldn't have to use it. We're not going that far."

"What d'ya mean 'we'?" Seth scoffed. "You got a mouse in your pack?" Then in a gentler voice, "I'm not going anywhere. Just gonna drop you off and head for home. 'Course, it would help if you tell me where we're going."

Travis finished fastening the packframe before responding. "Not far, about five or six miles up the Gunflint. I figure we can ride along shore to the end of the lake, then take the old road to the snowmobile trail. You know... the trail that follows along the blacktop. I want to be dropped off at a hiking path that winds back to Mystery Lake. Know where that is?"

"Yeah, I think I do," Seth said. "But you know, don't cha, that I can't use the snowmobile on that path without special permission. Part of it cuts through the Wilderness Area. Don't want to get caught like that dude last year. It cost him six hundred bucks plus his machine."

"The judge fined him six hundred big ones and still took his sled away? Whoa! Then be sure to stay on legal trails. Rollie would probably miss this expensive big toy, and you'd be too busy working off the fine to come out and mess around."

"You've got that right. You about ready? Then let's do it," Seth said, taking his place behind the handle grips. "Did you remember to bring a helmet?"

"Naw, don't need one. Watch your speed and steer away from trees. And if you do hit anything, I'll just use you as my crash dummy."

"Always with the funny mouth. Guess that's what happens when ya spend too much time alone. You start talking to yourself," Seth replied, pulling the starter cord. "Hang on! We're gonna head out."

Though the snow was thin and spotty, the large machine had little difficulty carrying two people and a bit of gear. Seth was an expert operator. A half hour later he had the snowmobile parked at the start of the hiking trail.

"Okay, my friend, this is it. You're on foot from now until tomorrow afternoon. So what time do you want your ride to be here?"

"Oh, great!" Travis blurted, after tugging up a sleeve to look at his wrist. "Wouldn't you know it! The battery on my watch seems to have bit the dust."

He removed a glove and tapped the crystal with a finger several times, hoping to bring new life to the now useless timepiece. "Dang! What do I do now? Hey, wait a minute. Did you wear yours this morning?"

"Nope. Guess you'll just have to use the sun." Seth said, pointing a gloved hand at the lemon-colored globe rising above the forest. "Why don't you start back about noon. You know when that is, don't cha? Just make sure that bright thing in the sky is due south. It'll be about time to head in."

"Clever, Seth, real cute. I'll be sure to remember the lesson. Big bright thing, sky, south. You know what? I think I've got it. Seriously, why don't we plan on meeting right here around three o'clock. That'll give me more time to fish. I'll start back around one or so. Shouldn't be more than a two hour hike."

"Okay," Seth agreed. "Meet you here around three. Sure you want to make it that late? Sunset's around four-thirty. If you get behind schedule, we'll be returning in the dark."

Travis grinned. "Then I'd be functioning a lot like you, wouldn't I? Your sister says you're usually in the dark 'bout most things. So I guess finding our way back home shouldn't be a problem. You probably do it all the time."

Seth threw his hands up in defeat. "Okay, okay! I give up. You win. But Trav, be careful and check the ice. Play safe, don't fall through."

"Hey! Would you get out of here! You're starting to sound like my mom."

"Oh, is that right? Then she must be one intelligent, interesting, and good-lookin' person." Seth boasted, readying himself to leave. "Have fun and good luck fishing. See ya tomorrow."

With that final remark, Seth cranked the engine, spun a one-eighty, and headed back the way he had just come.

Chapter Two

Alone in the quiet forest setting, the first thing Travis did was strap on his snowshoes. But, as he'd imagined, the snow was hard and unforgiving. After only a dozen careful steps he could see the wooden frames were taking abuse. He stopped, unhitched the bindings, and retied the shoes to the rear of the carrier.

As the sun rose and the morning warmed, so did Travis. Trekking while dressed in full winter gear was causing him to perspire. That meant inner clothing would be soaking up sweat. He was experienced enough to know this was definitely not a good thing. He'd be fine as long as he kept moving, but damp underwear wouldn't insulate him once he stopped for the day.

The youth trudged off the path, perched on a windfall, and took off the heavy outer jacket. Reaching inside his shirt confirmed his suspicions. The turtleneck was already moist.

The best thing to do, he decided, was to sit tight for a few minutes, let his body cool down. He was resting on the fallen tree, munching a breakfast bar, when a major mix-up popped into his head. Seth hadn't given him the freeze-dried food packets he'd promised to bring from the resort supply. And worse, Travis hadn't brought along any real grub—just a few snacks.

"How could I have been so careless?" Travis bellowed to every tree and bush within earshot. "Oh, man! It looks like another night with only fish on the menu."

Later that morning, as the teenager trudged the ups and downs of the trail, he was reminded of something he had known, but ignored. Distances on maps are deceiving. An inch on a chart is such a tiny space. Hiking that inch in real life can seem to take forever—especially if you're trekking with a loaded pack on your back.

Growing weary with so much walking, Travis stopped to check the chart. "Close, almost there. Mystery Lake can't be more than a block or two away," he mumbled to himself, folding the map and tucking it away.

Moments later, under a cloudless, robin-egg sky, he reached his destination. The teen stood with hands shielding his eyes, peering over a long, narrow lake, wishing he'd brought along sunglasses.

Before him lay a flat surface of white whose edges and beyond were outlined by forest covered hills fading up and into the distance. Scanning the shoreline, Travis concluded a spruce grove a few hundred yards away looked to be a great place to set up camp. There a grove of evergreens crowded close together; almost hugging the shore, providing protection should a wind arise.

The youth stepped cautiously onto the edge of the ice. Then, as he plodded along the rock-littered beach, he stomped a foot every three or four steps. The last thing Travis needed was a cold bath. He wanted to be certain the crusty surface, even next to the water's edge, would support his weight. Growing more confident with every stride, and anxious to get set up, he hurried his pace.

Perfect, he decided, spying an opening in the ever-greens. There was more than enough open space for a shelter and campfire. Travis slipped off the packframe and went right to work. Once the tent was pitched, he began preparing for evening.

The young man worked nonstop gathering wood. He had no trouble recalling how nights seemed to last an eternity when he had been stranded by the autumn windstorm. If fear and worry kept him wide awake, he wanted enough wood to keep a fire burning until morning's first light trickled over the horizon.

A cheerful mid-day sun smiled down while the fire-wood collection grew from a heap to a pile. Finally it was time to go fishing. "Look out you finny lunkers!" Travis yelled with youthful enthusiasm. "You're about to meet your maker!" Having said that, he pulled on his parka, gathered his tackle, and headed for the lake.

Though it would have been one more thing to carry, Travis wished he'd brought along his father's portable fish finder. The electronic gizmo would have located drop-offs where walleyes liked to hide. Without it, he'd just have to read the shoreline, and find a spot where the land dropped sharply into the water.

As it turned out, nearby was just such a place. A lava outcropping rose steeply from the water's edge, forming a rock-faced bluff. The water would be deep alongside the base of the cliff. With a short wooden-handled chisel in one hand, an ice rod in the other, and his head holding images of whopper-size walleyes, the young fisherman crunched his way along shore.

Arriving to where the cliff began its rise, Travis gingerly stepped farther out onto the lake surface. He bent and gave a whack with the stubby chisel. Safe. The ice held. The sharp blade hadn't punched through. He tramped farther away from shore and gave a second stroke.

It was fortunate the safety strap was wrapped around a wrist or the tool might have been lost. The razor sharp chisel slid through the ice as easily as if it had been thrust into a thin sheet of cardboard.

"Damn! Don't want an ice water swimming session," the startled teen cursed, standing frozen in place, the thin surface groaning beneath his feet. For several seconds all he could do was watch as dark water seeped through the cut and slowly stained a circle in the sparse snow cover.

Living next to a lake all his life, Travis knew this was a dangerous development. Obviously not all of the ice had a chance to form thick and strong before a late November storm had laid down several inches of white. The result of insulating snow, and unseasonably warm temperatures, had prevented ice from thickening. He'd have to be extremely cautious.

Barely lifting his feet, Travis shuffled back the way he'd come. A dozen careful slide steps later, he tried the chisel again. Better. The ice held. The first thrust didn't cut through. The surface where he was standing was several inches thick. It was strong enough to support his weight as long as he didn't stomp around with heavy feet. Travis knew—like it or not—this would be his fishing spot.

Once there was a foot-wide hole open for business, Travis pulled out a bait tin from one of the parka's pockets. He removed a small, dead minnow from the compact container and proceeded to bait a yellow lead-weighted hook. Then kneeling next to the hole, he plopped the hook and bait into water and began stripping line from the reel.

Yards and yards of clear monofilament slipped through the icy opening. The hopeful fish catcher was amazed at how much line had to be let out. He couldn't fathom it to be so deep—so close to shore. Eventually the lure struck bottom. Travis cranked the reel a few turns and began jigging the pole up and down. He was finally fishing.

As the afternoon wore on, the teen's shadow became longer, his feet grew colder, and there hadn't yet been a nibble on the bait. Off to the southwest, the sun was in the first act of calling it a day. The bright yellow ball was transforming itself into a red disc, soon to be hidden behind the forest-covered hill, leaving the young man in twilight.

A growling stomach reminded Travis nothing much had passed that way since before sunup. Without food packets, he desperately wanted to catch something—anything—to fill his empty belly. There were a few energy bars in the pack, but he thought best to save them for morning—or better yet—for the hike back to the highway.

Growing anxious, he knelt on one knee and doubled his efforts at jiggling the rod. Seconds later the pole was all but ripped from his grasp. From practice, he pushed the tip of the rod into the hole, waited a couple heartbeats, and then pulled back with a firm tug.

"All right!" Travis exclaimed, feeling a pulsing weight on the end of the line.

The young man had plenty of experience bringing in fish. He could tell from the way this fish fought that it was a real keeper, more than enough for a meal. Big enough to yield a pair of fine fillets. Enough, that after he fixed one fillet for supper, he'd have another to bring home.

Moments later a plump, golden-spotted fish lay flopping on the ice. But despite success, Travis wasn't smiling. This wasn't the whopper of a walleye he'd expected. Instead, he'd hooked a lake trout, the biggest he'd ever caught.

The hungry angler had a difficult decision. Lake trout season was closed. The season wouldn't reopen until mid-January. That meant, if he were to keep the fish, he'd be a poacher. Travis despised poachers. To him poachers were game hogs who had no respect for rules of fair play. He put them in the same category as week-old summer trash—they both stunk.

As he turned to face southwest, Travis witnessed the sun calling it a day, leaving the sky painted with bold streaks of reds and purples. Night came quickly this time of year. In moments it would be dark. There wasn't time to catch another meal. As he stood quiet, trying to make a decision, his stomach rumbled, urging him to keep the out-of-season supper.

"All right, maybe just this once," he mumbled, gathering up his things. With gear in one hand, the other holding the fish by the gills, Travis trundled toward camp.

Once back in the grove, he went right to work. Before going fishing, he'd placed birch bark and pine cones under a small stack of dead sticks. Within minutes of flicking the lighter, a crackling fire puffed up a plume of gray smoke.

Travis had plenty of practice cleaning fish. Fish had kept him alive when he had been stranded all alone back in October. He had said at the time he'd never want to eat one again. Right now the hole in his middle made that notion a fading memory. Using the longest blade of the survival tool, he carefully stripped the meat from the bones. He cut one fillet into smaller slabs, placed the pieces into a pan, and with the aid of several forked sticks, hung the pan over the fire. Soon the blended aroma of wood smoke and frying fish scented the air, making the boy's mouth water in hungry anticipation.

Although the fish was tasty, a slice of guilt took away some of the pleasure. Travis couldn't help wonder what would happen if the game warden learned about a big trout kept out of season. Maybe nothing, he thought. Maybe he'd only get a lecture not to do it again. Maybe it's all right to break the law when you don't have anything else to eat.

But Travis knew that was a pretty poor excuse. When he'd realized Seth hadn't given him any freeze-dried food packs, all he had to do was turn around and head for home. And since he hadn't remembered to ask, it was really his own fault he had to break the rules.

Finished with the one-course meal, Travis washed the pan in the snow, then added fuel to the fire. He sat close to its warmth, staring over the flames, thinking about his situation. The dilemma was the result of the autumn portage trip. His canoeing companion, Seth, had broken an ankle. Travis had to take on the role of caregiver. Without warning, the storm of the century blew over the Boundary Waters Canoe Area, trapping the two of them in a maze of tattered trees and stumps. After days of little to eat and dreadful weather, Travis decided to seek help. That decision proved to be a major mistake and almost proved fatal. Seth had been rescued. Travis hadn't been so fortunate.

Days of searching failed to find him. The rescue team thought he'd perished in the cold water of Brule Lake. His family even held a memorial service. But they had all been wrong. Though he'd been filled with dread and terror, and so very isolated, he'd managed to survive. It took ingenuity and a bit of luck, but he'd made his own escape.

Everyone, including the local newspaper reporter, heaped him with praise. 'Courageous and resourceful— kept his cool under stress.' Yeah, if they only knew, he thought. If people realized how terrified he'd been, they wouldn't think him so noble.

Once home, Travis had many sleepless nights. The question stuck in his mind like well-chewed gum to the underside of a desk: Would he ever again feel comfortable camping on his own? The fact was he loved the outdoors. But the fear he'd felt while trapped in the tattered forest lingered in his memory far worse than any nightmare ever had.

So he faked it. He'd told his folks this was to be a simple outing. Hike a few miles, do a little fishing, bed down overnight, head home the next day. A simple plan—an easy plan—especially with the string of beautiful winter days the region had been having.

His parents didn't question his motive. Why would they? They didn't know what was going on inside his head. The doubt and dread chewing holes in his self-confidence was something he had to fix on his own. If he were to conquer the fear demon lingering in his memory, he'd have to scare it away by himself.

Yet despite the terror he felt, he had experienced a valuable lesson. He'd learned that sometimes when things go wrong, you have no one to depend upon but yourself. And that's what he had done to survive.

The sudden 'who-who-hooting' of an owl interrupted Travis' thoughts—startling him. He had been gazing at the fire, not really seeing anything. Now he studied the lake opening and sensed a change taking place. Earlier, the black envelope overhead had been filled with a multitude of dazzling stars. Silently, mysteriously, they'd disappeared. That could only mean a cloud cover was moving over the Boundary Waters, closing an inky curtain on hopes for an entertaining display. There'd be no theater of northern lights to marvel at this evening.

"Oh, well," Travis sighed. "Who knows? Maybe it'll snow. Maybe I'll get to try out the snowshoes after all."

With that thought, he heaped wood on the fire, took one last look at the dark ceiling overhead, and crawled into his tent. The full day of fresh air and vigorous exercise had worn him out. Within minutes he fell into a deep sleep, putting his fears to rest. Not even the nearby howling of a Boundary Waters' timber wolf caused him to stir.

* * *

Seth didn't discover the mistake until he returned home. The ride back to the resort had been uneventful. Once there, he'd driven the snowmobile directly into the large garage used for storage and repair work. Seth was tugging at the rear of the machine, making certain the skis pointed toward the big door, when the oversight occurred to him.

His hand brushed across the closed flap of the rear storage compartment. The very same pocket he had tucked a small box of freeze-dried food packets. In the rush to send Travis on his way, he'd forgotten all about them.

Seth paused, hands resting on the lift bar, thinking what he should do about it. Nothing, he decided. There was nothing he could do. Travis was only going to be gone for one night. He had fishing gear, and possibly some snacks of his own in the pack. His buddy would be upset, but even if Trav didn't catch a fish, he certainly wouldn't starve missing a couple meals.

Seth resumed yanking the big machine into position for a quick departure the next day. When the Polaris was aimed at the door, he reached into the storage nook, grabbed the small box of powdered meals, and headed for the cottage.

Chapter Three

CHAPTER THREE

While Travis slumbered cozily in a warm winter sleeping bag, the weather began a foreboding change. A soft breeze had begun fanning from the east. Passing over the huge inland sea of Lake Superior, the atmosphere took on a full load of moisture.

Reaching the coastline, the foggy vapor was forced up and over the highlands of the Boundary Waters Wilderness Area. Cooled by the lifting, the air could no longer carry its load. When the moist blanket brushed against cold objects, everything touched turned frosty. Every tree and bush, every weed and rock, began wearing a white coat, making the world look as if it had been daintily dusted with powdered sugar. Eventually, when the landscape refused to accept another layer of frost, thick dense fog began to form.

Travis came awake just as the dull light of false dawn was seeping into the small shelter. He awoke rested, cheerful, and feeling good about himself. Congratulations were in order. He'd done it. He'd managed to keep his fears at bay. He'd slept the whole night through without once waking up. But now, having slept for so many hours, he had to get outside. Nature was calling.

He slithered out of the bag wearing only his long underwear and a pair of winter socks. First slipping into boots, he unzipped the tent door, then on all fours, crawled outside. The change took his breath away. In the murky predawn light the forest looked dressed for a wedding. Every needle, branch, and limb was sporting a fancy jacket of lacy white.

Travis stood with his back to the tent, answering his need. From where he was standing, the shoreline—only fifteen or twenty yards away—was almost impossible to see. Unless the fog cleared, he wouldn't dare go out on the ice. It'd be too easy to get confused—too easy to fall through and drown.

Completing his task, the teen crawled into the tent. Until the heavy air thinned, he would stay put. He hoped the thick pea soup wouldn't linger all day. If that happened, he'd have a difficult time finding his way to the blacktop. The best thing to do now was to crawl back in the bag. All he could do was wait.

Travis kicked off the boots, slid into the sleeping sack, and waited for the day to brighten. The shadowy light leaking through the tent fabric reminded him of mornings on the October trip. There had been day after day of low clouds and dreary damp weather. Surely the vapor today was just a morning fog—a fog that would burn off once the sun made its appearance. The forest around camp became covered by an eerie quiet; nothing stirred, not a sound could be heard. Travis had tucked his worry aside and had fallen back to sleep.

In the middle of a pleasant dream, the youth was jolted awake by a sharp boom. Still half asleep, he bolted upright in the bag, not sure what had caused the noise. A second shot shattered the quiet, the discharge sounding quite close to camp.

Alarmed, Travis practically jumped into his clothes. He scrambled through the tent door, pulling on his parka as he went. Outside, the fog had begun to lift. In the frosty silence the vapor hung suspended in tree tops, giving the forest an enchanted look often pictured in children's fairy tale books. Travis stood quiet, listening, not sure what to do. If the blasts had come from a poacher's gun, the last thing he wanted was to be seen.

If only his parka wasn't such a bright color. Its loud yellow fabric would show up like a billboard. The teen deliberated for a moment. Maybe there was a solution. He'd tucked the insulated vest in the packbag. The sleeveless jacket was camo-colored and would be much harder to spot. And though the air was damp, it was not terribly cold. A hat, gloves, and vest would provide enough warmth to do a little detective work.

The shots had come from the direction of the landing, the opening where he'd left the trail and had trudged along the ice. So that's the way he headed, keeping to the woods along the lake's edge—staying out of sight behind trees and brush.

Halfway to the entry path, he stopped and listened. Voices were drifting through the timber. Men, at least two of them, were talking. Travis was about to creep closer when another sound caught his attention. Something—or somebody—was coming his way. He needed to take cover—quick. Having left the spruce grove, he was standing in a mixed forest of birch, aspen, and cedar. None was big enough to hide behind.

The light scrunch of footsteps drew closer. Travis caught a glimpse of movement off to one side—something dark, low to the ground. At first sighting, he thought it might be a fisher or pine martin, dusky-furred mammals of northern forests. The creature passed an opening, giving the youth a better look. He had guessed wrong. The animal wasn't what he'd first thought. It was a small wolf—a jet-black yearling—limping along on three legs.

Anger boiled up in the teenager like soup on a hot stove. Wolves were protected by both federal and state regulations. Only a real outlaw would chance shooting such an animal. The pup passed by, completely unaware of the boy's presence, its ebony fur vanishing behind frost-covered brush.

Travis returned his attention to the voices. The men were having a heated exchange of words, but they were still too far away to be heard clearly. Though risky, he needed to get closer. He wanted to know more.

Slowly, step by step, tree by tree, Travis moved toward the talking, stopping every few feet to test his ears. When he could understand most of the words, he dropped to his knees and scurried behind a windfall.

Peering over the log, he spied two people, both with beards. One man tall and thin—sharp knees and elbows. The second man short and round—a red-whiskered Dough Boy. Each wore dingy white coveralls. They were bent at the waist, working. On the ground between them was a soft mound of gray. Travis couldn't believe his eyes. The men were skinning a wolf—a mature Boundary Waters' timber wolf.

A sudden wave of dread swept over Travis, causing his heart to race and his hands to shake. How bold could these guys be? The penalty for wolf poaching would be thousands of dollars, maybe even jail time. He knew for certain he wouldn't want to be seen. If these men could be so casual about killing wolves, what would they do to a teenager caught spying on them?

Alarmed and unsure what to do, Travis remained hidden, plotting strategy. Even with a heart pounding like a jack hammer, he tried to stay still. More conversation filtered through the frost-coated forest. The first words arrived in a squeaky voice.

"How hard could it be to follow? I'm sure you hit it. There must be a blood trail."

The quick reply was raspy and rude. "That'd be stupid. We could lose hours chasing after it. Soon as we finish skinning this critter, we should probably make tracks ourselves."

Squeaky voice disagreed. "Yeah, but what if it didn't go far? That black coat could bring us a nice chunk of change."

"Maybe, but you'd just blow your share on booze. I think the best bet is to ditch this critter's carcass and get out of here. We're history if we get caught with this pelt. I don't know 'bout you, but I ain't got enough cash to cough up for bail."

Travis was furious. Shooting a wolf just to sell the hide for a few dollars went against everything he'd been taught.

The raspy voice continued. "OK, that's it. I'll roll up the skin and put it in my pack. You better cover the remains in the woods. Make sure you put it on the other side of the trail where no one will ever find it."

Footsteps crunched in the boy's direction. Travis raised up to take a quick glance. The pudgy fellow was backing toward the blowdown. The man was clutching the rear legs of the naked wolf, dragging the lifeless form directly toward Travis. The youth felt his heart rise to his throat. He was certain he'd be seen.

The out-of-shape poacher was so near Travis could hear wheezing as the man sucked in air. Just when Travis thought it was over, that he'd meet the same fate as the animal, the raspy voice boomed through the forest. "Hey Rusty! Did ya see these footprints? They lead down to the ice. You better get your butt over here. We need to check 'em out."

"What are ya barkin' about? I didn't see any tracks," the stout man chirped, almost in Travis' ear. "What direction they headed?"

"Looks like they go along the lake. Somebody musta come this way. Break down the rifle and hide it away. No sense taking chances. It might be a warden."

"Yeah, good idea," came the reply, the high-pitched voice fading as the man returned to the kill site.

Travis let out his breath. Now what? What if the poachers decided to follow his footprints? They were sure to find the tent. But what should he do about it? Maybe, for the time being, he should just stay put. Maybe it was best to wait, find out what the poachers were going to do first.

He huddled on the ground, positive the men could hear his heart hammering. That's when the snow began. He'd focused only on the poachers and hadn't noticed the fog lifting. Magically, as if commanded by a wave of a wand, large, wet, butterfly flakes filled the air. In no time at all Travis became invisible—coated like the forest—in a layer of white.

Within a moment or two, cold, damp air began seeping through his shirt and vest. He had dressed warm enough for walking, but lying motionless on the snowy ground was making him shiver. Like it or not, he had to move.

His muscles had already begun to stiffen and Travis had to force himself to sit up. Snow was now falling in earnest. Almost as if a pillow had been ripped open, feather-sized flakes filled the air. Chilled and nervous, but needing to know the poachers' plans, Travis decided he had no choice but to follow behind.

The teen moved cautiously away from the log. New snow helped silence footsteps and he knew that was a good thing. As if playing hide and seek, he silently stalked closer to the lake. The men hadn't gone far. They were holding a conference about the footprints. Travis crouched behind a tree to listen.

The mismatched pair were only yards away, but dressed in white, they appeared ghostly, blending with the background. The stout man was doing the talking—his voice as irritating as the cry of an unattended infant.

"I don't care if someone might be camped 'round here. I'm getting out while the gettin's good. We got what we come for. Nobody's seen us. This new snow will cover our tracks. What we waitin' on?"

"Think, you idiot!" the lean man bellowed. "What if someone did see us? How do ya know they're not hiding and waitin' for us to go—follow us up the trail?"

"Look, man! It's one thing to shoot a critter. It's something else when you're dealin' with a person. I don't want any part of it. I'm leaving."

"Tell ya what," the thin poacher said, placing a hand on the portly man's soft shoulder. "Let's just have a little look-see along the lake. What can it hurt? We'll still have plenty of time to ski out to the machines. With this new snow covering our tracks, who'd be the wiser?"

"Oh cripes, I don't know." There was a pause before the squeaky voice continued. "Oh...I 'spose. I'll help ya look for a couple minutes. But if we do come across someone, don't be doin' something stupid."

"Course not. What kind of fool ya think I am? We'll just tell 'em we were skiing the trail when we heard a couple of gun shots. We'll play innocent—find out what they know. Come on. Let's walk along the lake and see what we find."

Travis looked on in silence as the man slipped his arms into a large packsack, patted his portly friend on the back, and stepped onto the ice. Now what? He could wait until they passed, then head for the path, start jogging to the blacktop. But that would mean he'd have to leave his gear. He didn't want to have do that. And what if they only searched for a few minutes? He'd heard them say they had skis stashed. Grown men on skis would easily catch up to him.

Shivering with cold, he had to move. Angry at being placed in this awkward position by a pair of scofflaws, Travis wanted to observe the men—see if they would discover his tent. He was surprised when he glanced down. Recent footprints were already hidden by large flakes. That meant his tracks along shore would be getting covered, be almost impossible to recognize. When walking along shore the day before, the snow had been hard and crusty. He hadn't sunk in far. This fresh snow burst should quickly conceal the shallow prints.

Filled with nervous dread, Travis crept carefully from tree to tree, angling closer to the lake's edge. With snow falling faster, he could scarcely see the poachers as they trudged along the shoreline. The men were almost to the evergreen stand. When they paused, Travis did the same. From his hiding spot, it looked like the two were having another argument. The short fellow was waving his hands in the air like a band conductor directing a fast-paced tune, obviously angry and trying to get his point across. Then, suddenly whirling, the stubby little man pointed toward the landing.

It appeared to Travis that the poachers were looking directly at him. They must be able to see me, he thought, staying motionless behind a birch clump. He stayed statue-still until the men looked the other way— the tall man pointing in the general direction of the evergreen stand.

Through the milky gauze of falling snow, Travis could just make out the red-whiskered poacher shaking his head. Suddenly the man spun around and started shuffling back the way he had just come. Oh-oh, Travis shuddered. He's going to walk right by here. Moving an inch at a time, the nervous spy forced himself flat to the ground. Then he rolled over, put his face in the snow, and tried to stop breathing.

The fat fellow tramped by only yards away from the birch clump hiding spot. The man was so close; Travis could hear him wheezing for breath—as if walking took lots of extra effort. Lifting up on one elbow, he watched as the man lumbered away. And suddenly, like a spirit, the rotund figure faded into the background, disappearing from view.

Breathing a little easier, heart still racing, Travis twisted toward the lanky fellow. He too, had vanished, the light colored coveralls invisible in a field of white. What now? Travis tried to picture where he'd set up the tent. Would the man spot it from the shore ice? Maybe not. The tent was green, almost the color of spruce trees. By now the nylon shell would be coated with snow. So, unless one knew where to look, the little shelter should be about impossible to see.

A chill overtook the youth, causing him to shudder. His knees and elbows were damp from sliding around on the ground, and although the temperature was holding around the freezing mark, Travis knew he had to return to camp. He'd need the parka, and if snow kept falling, maybe even the snowshoes. Events weren't following his schedule. This simple fishing trip was becoming much more of an adventure than he had imagined when he'd left home.

* * *

That same morning Mrs. Larsen heard the alarm to go off for the second time. The clinic where she worked would open soon. She needed to get ready or risk being late. Her husband had left for Duluth long before daylight. He was scheduled to be the featured speaker at a one-day conservation conference being held in the port cities. Now she wished he could have put off the speech until Travis had returned.

She stood at the bedroom window, staring over the lake. Through the frosty glass the world outside appeared alien. Thick as wood smoke, fog hung suspended over the house and yard, blotting out the usual scenic view of Poplar Lake. What Linda Larsen could see was covered with white ice crystals—every object dipped in vanilla frosting. Even the wrought iron deck chairs appeared foreign, their normally skinny legs now fat and pregnant-looking.

Mrs. Larsen had stayed up to catch the forecast on the late night news. 'No change for the next couple of days,' the weather woman promised. No mention of fog. Linda felt like calling the station, asking the lady if she had been talking about Arizona or some other warm weather state. Because outside this windowpane, there wasn't a hint of a promise for 'another sunny day.'

As a mother, she couldn't help being worried. They'd all thought Travis had drowned while on the canoe trip. She didn't want to think about having to go through an experience like that again. Once was more than enough, thank you.

The worried woman stood staring through the glass, wondering if there was anything she could do for her son. He couldn't be reached by phone. Cell phones didn't work this far up the Gunflint. And besides, Trav hadn't taken one along. As she turned toward the clothes closet, Linda couldn't help but think that maybe the boy's father was right. Maybe she did worry too much. Travis knew how to take care of himself. He'd be okay.

Right now she needed to get ready for work and get on the road. The misty blanket outside would slow her trip to the clinic. Then she had a second thought: Beth would be home all day. The ten-year-old could call if there was any news. In any event, Travis wasn't due home until dark. The fog should be long gone by then. And if needed, she could contact the rangers—maybe get permission for Seth to pick Travis up along the hiking trail. Feeling a bit better, she grabbed a white uniform off a hanger and finished dressing.

Chapter Four

C H A P T E R   F O U R

Though he couldn't see the man, Travis wanted to stay hidden on the return trip to the tent. He angled away from the lake, hoping to find a trace of earlier footsteps. Too much new snow had fallen. Prints were already covered. Now he had to be extra cautious. The white-out was blurring the landscape, making it easy to get confused. With a thick coat of frost, and sticky new snow, every tree and bush was a twin. He paused for a moment. It was probably best to return to the birch clump. As long as he stayed near the lake, he shouldn't get lost.

That proved to be a wise decision. Footprints made only moments earlier were quickly filling in. Back at the birch cluster, Travis peered out at the white sheet cloaking the lake. What he didn't see was the long-legged poacher. And knowing that he needed to keep moving to chase away the chills, Travis began the trek to camp. He stalked from tree to tree like a military scout, continually keeping an eye out for the enemy.

The youth exhaled a soft sigh of relief. He'd made it to the spruce grove without a seeing any sign of the wolf killer. Just ahead the evergreens were closely spaced, hanging heavy and low with wet snow. Perfect, he thought; the little shelter would be well hidden. Nervous, pulse pounding, Travis crept into the grove, hesitating every few feet to look and listen. Nothing— only the rasp of his breathing and rustle of his snowmobile bibs whenever he moved.

Drawing close, he slowed even more, taking one gentle step at a time. The camp opening lay just ahead and was like he'd pictured: the tent blended with the background, its green fabric sagging under the weight of a fresh coating of white.

Travis again paused, looking for man tracks. Satisfaction—there weren't any. He sprinted to the tent, unzipped the door, and clambered inside. What he needed to do now was to crawl into the bag and warm up.

* * *

The long-limbed poacher was puzzled. The faint footprints he had been trailing had disappeared. With flakes falling fast and furious, the man could barely see the forest bordering the lake's edge, much less day-old boot tracks. He had another concern. How safe was the lake surface? The snow burst was putting an extra strain on it, causing the thin ice to crack and moan. Lake water was seeping through, turning snow to thick slush, making walking difficult.

He had promised his partner he'd be back within the hour. Since the search was proving pointless, the man decided to head back to the landing. The safest route would be right along the shore—no sense getting feet wet.

Travis was crawling into his sleeping bag about the time the poacher stopped in front of the spruce thicket. The rangy fellow hadn't noticed the open space when he had passed by earlier. He knew a good camping site when he saw one. This was a perfect place to pitch a tent, surrounded as it was by a wall of evergreens. And something looked out of place. Through the snowy haze, the outlaw spotted the circular mound of the shelter.

Travis had blundered. In his rush to get inside, he'd bumped the slick nylon fabric. A bit of the camouflaging snow had lost its grip. Even in the near whiteout conditions, the dome shaped little dwelling looked unfamiliar and out of place parked between the triangular shaped trees. Unfortunately for Travis, the poacher's curiosity was aroused. The scofflaw shrugged off his pack, set it on the lakeshore, and walked silently toward the tent.

Travis had just made himself comfortable when the shelter suddenly shook. In a voice the young man would never forget, came the gruff command. "You there, in the tent, come on out! We need to talk."

Fear and dread flooded over Travis as if he'd been swept over a falls. The teen was petrified—didn't know what to do—so he did nothing—hoping the man would go away. But the poacher had spotted the boy's tracks. One set, fresh, coming from the direction of the landing.

Again came the raspy speech, only this time in a gentler tone. "Come on out, nothing to fear. Just want to know if ya heard a couple of gun shots 'bout an hour ago."

Travis somehow found his voice. In a high chirp he managed to reply, "I didn't hear anything. I just woke up."

"Oh, that right? Then who's been walking around your tent, Frosty the Snowman? Come on out. We need to have a chat. Ya got nothin' to be afraid of. I ain't gonna hurt ya."

Scared out of his wits, and not thinking clearly at all, Travis squeaked out a reply. "You're gonna get in trouble mister, so why don't you just leave?"

"Right! Trouble, huh? Maybe you've got that reversed. Maybe you're the one that's gonna have a problem. Now, you gonna get out here or am I gonna have to drag ya out?"

Travis, thinking the man would do just that, stammered out a response. "I'll come out. Just give me a minute to get my boots on." But that was easier said than done. The teen was shaking so badly he couldn't get his feet to cooperate.

The poacher was running out of patience. "Hurry up! I ain't got all day."

"I'm trying. I'm trying. I gotta get dressed." Several long moments later Travis emerged from the tent looking small and frightened.

"Well, blazes, you ain't nothing but a boy. What you doin' out here all by yourself? Didn't your folks ever tell ya nasty things can sometimes happen to kids when they're far away from home?"

For the first time, Travis looked directly at the poacher. The guy wasn't exactly ugly, but the unkempt beard and greasy hair poking out from his stocking cap made the man look a little like a cartoon character. The outlaw was looking down at Travis. For fourteen, Travis was tall. But this man towered over him. He was even taller than Travis' father who stood well over six feet.

However, unlike his dad, this creep had narrow shoulders and hollow cheeks—as if he might be in need of dental work. The man grinned and Travis could see he'd thought right. Several of the poacher's teeth were missing, creating black holes, twisting his evil smile into a jack-o-lantern smirk.

From down deep, Travis plucked up a bit of hidden courage. "I'm careful. I only came out here to do some fishing. I'm about to pack up and head for home."

"Some fishing, hey? Show me what ya got in the tent. Maybe there's something I can use."

For a brief moment the boy's anger overcame his fear, pushing common sense aside. "Look, why don't you just turn around and leave? There's no way I'll catch up. You can ski to wherever you parked your snowmobiles and be long gone before I get back to the highway."

Travis realized too late that he'd said too much. Now the jerk knew he'd been spying—knew he'd seen them skinning the wolf. New fright filled the pit of his otherwise empty stomach.

"Oh, is that right? Sounds like you know a lot more than what's good for you. But kid, you don't listen so well. I told you to get your gear out here. I wanna have a look."

"Get it yourself!" Travis snapped, sorry at once he had yelled.

"Okay, I will." With that, the poacher cuffed Travis hard on the shoulder, knocking the teenager off his feet. "Ya oughta learn how to talk to your elders, kid. Ya might run into someone who takes offense at being yapped at like that."

The would-be thief took several quick steps toward the tent, dropped to his knees, and peered through the door. "Nice cozy setup. It's even got a floor. Well lookee' here! You got all kinds of good things," the man said, dragging the packframe into the open. "Guess you were telling the truth. You were fishing. Catch anything?"

"What do you care? It's none of your business." Travis muttered, eyes fixed on the laces on his boots.

"Well, you're wrong. You see, the way I figure, I can't let you trail us out. My friend and I need a little time to make our get-away. I don't see any food, though. So I guess if you're gonna stay out another night, you'll need to be a pretty good fisherman."

"You'd make me stay out another night?" Travis stuttered, looking up into the man's dark beady eyes. "That's a mistake. My family will send someone to get me."

"I'll say one thing for you. For a kid, ya got a lot of spunk. And you're right. I can't leave you here. Start packing."

"Why? I can wait until later. I won't be able to tell anyone until tonight. You can be far from here by then," Travis protested, his voice almost a whine.

"Yeah, maybe so. But ya know what? I ain't gonna chance it. Now start breaking camp or I'll have to do something to let ya know I'm serious."

The frightened youth crawled inside, rolled up the sleeping bag, and stuffed it into the carrier pouch. Once outside, he secured it to the packframe, and then started brushing snow from the tent fabric. This was a small domed tent that used folding rods for support. The teen had always marveled how tiny and compact the shelter became when packed properly. But now, being so nervous, he didn't think he could roll it tight—make it small enough to fit into its carry sack. Taking a quick glance over his shoulder, Travis saw the poacher inspecting one of the snowshoes.

"Say kid, these are pretty fancy. Where'd ya buy 'em?"

"I didn't. I made them myself," Travis snapped. "They're special. Leave them alone."

"No, don't think so. I always wanted a pair of pretty wooden shoes. Carry some cheap little 'luminum jobs with me when I snowmobile in deep powder. These here are a whole lot nicer. Think I'll keep them as a gift. After all, I'm being a good guy. I'm gonna let ya go—not gonna hurt a hair on your handsome head."

"So go, but leave the shoes. They're too small for you anyway."

The man removed a tattered glove and scratched his beard in thought. "Yeah, I think you're right. They probably are too small. And I guess I wouldn't want the law to question me if I was in possession of any of your stuff. That'd be pretty hard to explain."

Travis found it difficult to watch as the poacher placed the shoes on the snow, and then stomped on them. The sound of splitting wood made the boy wince.

"There!" the man announced, holding up the snow-shoes for Travis to see. "You can keep 'em, but I don't think they'll work too well. Do you?"

Travis glared before reaching out and ripping the shoes from the man's outstretched hands. Broken or not, they were his. Maybe he could fix them once he was home.

"Now then," the man said, once again showing off his Halloween smile. "The way I figure it, you can identify me. So to encourage that memory to fade some, we'll need to take a little hike."

New terror filled every fiber of the teen's body. If Travis hadn't already emptied his bladder, he was sure he would have wet his underwear. This creep wasn't going to hurt him. Instead, the man was going to get him lost, and then leave him in the woods like in the Hansel and Gretel fairytale. Only Travis wouldn't have any pebbles or bread crumbs. He'd be on his own in the middle of nowhere, not knowing which way was home.

"You're movin' too slow. We gotta get going." The scofflaw snatched the tent from the boy's hands. He stuffed the poles and tent into the tent sack, hitched it to the packframe, and held it out for Travis to take.

"Put it on. We gotta leave," the man demanded. "I've wasted enough time foolin' around with you. You're wearing out my goodwill."

Dropping to his knees, Travis somehow managed to tie the now useless snowshoes to the other gear. He slipped into the backpack straps and stood quiet—afraid to move. The poacher had stalked to where the fire had been built—surplus wood now covered with a blanket of snow.

"No sense leaving this," the poacher said. "It's much too easy for someone to find. It'd be a good clue that you were once here." The man started kicking at the pile, scattering leftover fire sticks in all directions. Close to the snow-filled ash heap his foot uncovered the clear storage bag containing the fish fillet.

The poacher plucked up the sack and held it to the light. "Well, now. I've been fishin' these parts most of my life. I know a lake trout fillet when I see one. You ain't no better than me, boy. Trout season don't open up around here for a couple of weeks yet. This here is a poached fish. You got some nerve tellin' me I'm the one in trouble. I'd say we're two of a kind." With that, he grunted out a loud horse laugh and flung the bag far over the evergreens.

Returning to Travis, the poacher wrinkled his forehead and puckered his lips as if thinking was a difficult task, then asked, "You got a scarf in that packsack of yours? We need something to cover your eyes."

"What? Why? Can't see much anyway the way it's snowing."

"Boy, you ask too many fool questions. But I'm gonna tell ya anyway. See, I figure if you're blindfolded, there'll be no need to stroll so far into the forest. Just lookin' out for your best interest. Now, ya got one or not?"

"Ahh…there's a stocking cap mask in my pocket. Will that work?"

"Well now, that's more like it. Put it on, but put it on backwards. You and me are about to take a little nature hike. Just pretend it's one of those snipe hunts kids do at summer camp. Heck, you might even enjoy it."

Travis did as he was instructed, tugging the cap over his head so eye openings faced the rear. He stumbled and almost fell as the man gave him an abrupt shove forward. Then the poacher placed a hand on the boy's shoulder and began guiding the teen deeper into the forest. For the next twenty minutes no words were exchanged. Drawing alongside a small aspen tree, the poacher suddenly jerked Travis to a halt.

"This should be far enough. Lose the pack, but keep the cap on," the raspy voice demanded. "Now I'm truly sorry for what I'm about to do. But ya gotta understand my situation here. If I were to just walk away, you could follow my tracks. I gotta make sure you're gonna be tied up for a while as it were. At least until some snow covers my trail."

The outlaw pushed Travis so the boy's back was against the trunk of the tree. The man reached into a coverall pocket and pulled out a length of bailing twine. Next, he pulled Travis' arms back until the youth's hands were behind and on opposite sides of the sapling.

"Here's what I figure. This cord ain't all that strong, but it's too tough for you to break in one pull. What ya wanna do is keep rubbing it up and down on the tree. Before long you'll start to pop some of them stringy fibers. After an hour or two, you should have enough missing that ya can break loose."

Travis hardly heard a word. He had never been so terri-fied. This creep was crazy, tying him up in the middle of the woods. The only chance was to somehow talk his way out of the dilemma. In a voice close to tears, Travis

41

stammered, "Mister, you can't leave me here. That's like murder. Someone's sure to find out."

"Oh, kid, don't cha see the beauty of it? Think of it as a test. You're gonna be able to break free in a little while. Then all ya gotta do is get back to the lake. Heck, you can set up that fancy little tent and enjoy the afternoon fishin' if ya like. Wait for that help you said would be coming along. But, on the other hand, it ain't my fault if some fool kid gets lost in an unexpected snowstorm."

"I told you the truth. My friend will be at the landing in a little while. He was supposed to meet there this morning," Travis lied, struggling to break the cord.

"Well then, ya just better hope he don't come too soon. You wouldn't want your friend to have an unexpected accident—would ya?"

That shut Travis up. Blindfolded and bound, he was already near full panic. He'd experienced panic often on the fall trip. If he'd learned anything, it was that panic was a person's number one enemy. If he was going to be able to escape and survive, he'd somehow have to keep panic from making him crazy—keep him from doing foolish things. He forced himself to relax and breathe deep. He'd just have to wait for the lunatic to leave.

Travis sensed that the poacher was standing close. Body odor and bad breath filtered through the mask. The youth recoiled with fear as the man started searching parka pockets.

"Well, now," the poacher uttered so close Travis could taste the man's stinky breath. "I better take this little red fire starter with me. Already found those waterproof matches ya had tucked in that tiny tackle box. If you plan on having a fire, I guess you'll just have to rub two sticks together." The man gave a laughing grunt next to the teen's ear and moved away.

The next thing Travis heard was a branch breaking. Blindfolded, he couldn't see the poacher shuffling backwards, using a spruce bough like a broom, filling in footprints. "Take your time," came a muted suggestion, the snow muffling the man's unusual voice. "It's still early. Ya got all day."

As Travis stood shaking with fear and frustration, tears sliding down his cheeks, everything went quiet. Not even the soft breeze puffing at the tree tops made a sigh. It was as if the world was suddenly without sound.

* * *

Linda Larsen barely made it to work on time. Fog had blanketed the highway for most of the twenty-five mile trip down the Gunflint. It wasn't until her car crested the huge hill overlooking Grand Marais that the air cleared. Later, while gazing out the clinic window, she wondered what the weather was like at home.

Water in Lake Superior remains nearly the same temperature all year around. The lake is so large that during the winter season it often keeps the coastline milder than farther inland. It is not uncommon for thermometers in town to read ten or fifteen degrees warmer than thermometers just over the small mountain. Mrs. Larsen wondered if the inland sea was playing that temperature trick now.

Deep in thought, she stared at trickles of mist snaking down the glass, speculating if it was snowing at home. At break she'd call Beth and find out. Mother's intuition was nagging at her inner voice, telling her that Travis was in trouble.

The clinic door opened and a patient walked in. Startled, Mrs. Larsen turned from the window. She had to get back to business.

Chapter Five

C H A P T E R   F I V E

Travis was trying to follow the man's advice. He was pulling hard on the twine, attempting to scrape the thin cord against the sapling. For the first few minutes he'd been too terrified to do anything. He'd just stood with his back tight to the tree, sniffling, unable to keep his eyes and nose from leaking.

Eventually, when his tears slowed, he pushed panic to one side and went to work. What the man said made sense. Just like the fabled mouse that freed the lion, the cord could be cut—one strand at a time.

The first problem was making his arms go up and down. They were in an awkward position. Held tight by the twine, Travis was unable to move his limbs more than a few inches in either direction. After a few minutes of struggling, his shoulder sockets begged for relief. The pain was so unbearable he was forced to stop. He sagged his head against the tree, deep in thought. Maybe knee-bends. He could hold his arms in one position, and let his legs do the work.

As he leaned forward, a small section of stocking cap momentarily clung to the tree. A light bulb switched on. Travis rose up on his toes, pressed his head back, and slowly lowered himself. Fabric snagged on the tree's bark causing the rear of the stocking cap to ride up a few inches.

He repeated the action until material had clumped itself high on the back of his skull. Then, after a brief rest, he did the same trick with the left side of his face. Slowly the cloth walked its way up his cheek. The fabric finally climbed past one eye, then the other. A little less panic—he could see again.

Snow was falling, if anything, harder than when he had left camp. And Travis noticed something else. It was a dryer snow. The flakes tumbling down on his nose and eyelashes were no longer plump and wet. This was a type of snow that could accumulate, and if a wind picked up, tumble into drifts.

What Travis didn't see were the tracks they'd made while walking in—only a few were visible near his tie-down tree. Others had vanished. How was that possible? He didn't have the answer, and he didn't have time to think about it. At the moment he had more important things to be concerned about.

With vision reclaimed, some of the terror diminished—replaced by anger and frustration. Travis began frantically working the twine up and down. After fifteen or twenty rubs he would lunge forward, hoping the cord would snap, but that hadn't happened. Part of the problem was not being able to tug with full strength. Pulling with all his might put too much stress on his arm and shoulder joints, causing severe pain.

The strenuous work warmed him, and though perspiring profusely, he kept at it. Up and down, up and down—until legs howled and shoulders burned. Every minute or two he'd pause, lean back, take in large gulps of air, and begin again.

When he least expected, Travis broke free. He'd just started a tug when the twine snapped, causing him to fall face first to the ground. For a moment he stayed quite still, savoring the small victory, enjoying the sensation of cold flakes cooling his sweaty face.

After a time he rolled over, crawled to the tree, and sat with his back to the trunk. Taking off a glove, Travis dug into his snowmobile bibs. There, deep in an inside pocket, snuggled the leather-cased survival tool. The gadget had been a surprise present from his parents. The tool, and the compass that came with it, had been extremely useful when Travis had been trapped by the autumn storm. He opened a knife blade, cut twine from his wrists, and stuffed the cord in a pocket. He might find some use for it later.

Then he sat stone-still, staring off into the forest, thinking over the morning's events. The autumn experience had proved to be a tremendous teacher. One of the most valuable lessons learned was to plan. When faced by a dilemma, and if time permits, planning, not panic, helped find a solution.

He needed to reconstruct the morning—to put a time frame on each activity. What time had he heard the shots? How long had he spied and followed the poachers? How much time was spent walking in the woods? Finally, how long had he been tied to the tree?

Adding it all up, Travis figured the whole ordeal couldn't have taken more than two or three hours. The wolf killer had been right. Most of the day still lay ahead. Pleased there was plenty of daylight left, Travis pondered the next problem. Without knowing which direction they'd gone going in, how was he going to walk out?

He unzipped his jacket, reached under the rim of his turtleneck, and exposed a cotton cord. He pulled on the

46

string until a shiny half dollar sized object popped into the open. This was the second part of the gift. A compass with an inside cover containing a flat strip of flint.

Travis had discovered the magical fire-starting material by accident. When stranded by the windstorm, he had been surviving on raw fish because he had lost his lighter. Lying inside the tent one rainy afternoon, he found that the back of the compass case could be unscrewed.

He thought it weird that a narrow piece of gray flat stone was glued to the inside. But the more he mulled it over, the more he realized the mineral was put there for a purpose. Eventually Travis made the connection that the survival tool and compass had come together in a kit. They were designed to work with each other. He knew that striking steel on flint makes sparks. The first fire hadn't come easy, but once Travis learned the technique, he practiced until he had it mastered.

Cupping the compass in the palm of his hand, he wondered if this unique gift would again be the key to survival. He pushed himself up, brushed off his parka, and pulled out the folded map the poacher had thankfully overlooked. The colorful chart confirmed his thinking. He'd set up camp on the northwest edge of Mystery Lake. And now, if he wanted to return to the evergreen grove, the trek would have to be on a southeasterly course.

Travis located the campsite. He moved his finger away from the lake in several directions, and then slid it forward in a southeasterly heading. The first two attempts brought the finger back to the shores of the lake. The third time he drew back in a more westerly motion and then knew what was bothering him.

If the poacher had walked him west, it was possible to miss the lake altogether if now he were to head southeast. With snow falling faster by the minute, it'd be easy to cross the narrow trail without ever seeing it. And if that happened, he'd be completely lost. There'd be no way of knowing where he was or which way to go.

To be certain to connect somewhere along the lake, he'd have to walk on a more easterly heading. Though the lake was narrow, it was several miles long. Even if he reached far up shore from the campsite, it'd be safer than missing the lake altogether.

Travis was about to slip into the packframe when his stomach growled. The morning's activities had been so frightening he'd forgotten about missing meals. Three bars remained hidden near the bottom of the pack. He decided it was time to munch one before heading out. He savored each bite, and although the treat tasted terrific, the small snack did little to ease the hunger pains gnawing away at his middle.

Almost ready to depart, Travis held the compass against his chest, slowly rotated his feet until the needle and north were aligned, and then did a quarter turn to the right. He was now facing east. Under ordinary conditions, he would have selected a target object. That wouldn't work well today. Snow bursts obscured the landscape. Distant features disappeared in a wall of bleached white. Travel would be at a snail's pace.

It didn't take long to realize walking was now an arduous task. Snow hadn't been deep when the outlaw had forced him into the forest. Travis now found every step required extra effort. The quilt was becoming thicker by the minute. High stepping was hard work. The warm parka would have to come off or he'd soon be soaked.

After packing away the jacket, Travis stood motionless. The world around him was hushed. The only sound was the whoosh of his breathing. For a moment he wondered about this strange happening and thought he knew the reason why. The quiet was the result of soft flakes coating every tree, bush, and rock. Noise had nowhere to go. Sounds were trapped, and then he theorized, if I don't get moving, I'll be trapped with them.

He had been trudging for more than an hour when doubt began creeping into his brain. For sure he wasn't walking nearly as fast as when they'd gone in. But that hike hadn't lasted long—no more than twenty or thirty minutes. So by now, if the heading was accurate, he should have reached the lake.

What Travis didn't know, sightless as he had been on the trip into the forest, was that his captor hadn't taken him all that far. That now, traveling east, the course was leading to Mystery Lake at a wide angle. He'd eventually stumble upon its banks, but he'd arrive far up shore from the campsite. He took a bearing and plodded on, fingers crossed that he was doing the right thing. He'd only taken a few steps when he caught a glimpse of movement. Startled, and without a moment's hesitation, Travis scampered behind a tree. And although his heart was racing, curiosity got the best of him. He chanced a peek. Coming his way, looking exhausted and near death was the black-furred young wolf.

The immature animal labored to make progress, unaware of being watched. Travis stayed still, surprised that the pup could move at all. Shot high in the hindquarters, the small predator was pulling itself forward using only its front paws. Like a pair of oars in an empty boat, the rear legs dragged uselessly behind.

Travis looked on in horror. When the wolf was only a few feet away, it stopped, put its head on its paws, and closed its eyes. "No! Don't you dare die in front of me!" Travis mouthed without sound. "Don't you dare die!"

Long moments passed. The youth stood silent, angry, and perplexed while the animal agonized to catch its breath. What now, Travis wondered. He couldn't just

walk away, and let the animal suffer. The young outdoorsman had seen his father approach wolves trapped
for wildlife research—slow and low: Never making
threatening gestures—always speaking in a gentle tone
of voice. Trying the same technique, Travis began talking. "It's all right little guy. I'm not gonna hurt you.
You're gonna be okay."

The animal jerked its head up at the first syllable. A
growl rose from deep within its throat. Undaunted,
Travis kept speaking, sensing he had nothing to fear.
The wolf wasn't going anywhere. And as long as he
kept clear of its jaws, the predator couldn't hurt him.

After a long one-sided conversation, the growling
slowed and eventually quit. Then, as if too tired to do
anything else, the pup dropped its muzzle to its paws
and lay quiet.

"I guess we both have our troubles," Travis acknowl-
edged, his voice soothing as a late night DJ's. "You can't
walk and I'm not sure where I am. So what are we
gonna do about it?"

Travis shrugged off the pack and leaned it against the
tree. He dropped to his knees, pulled out the parka,
and rolled it in a ball. Then slowly, inch by inch, he
crept closer to the wolf, jacket held at arms length,
words smooth as silk.

He approached cautiously from the rear, keeping the
parka out front—just in case. Travis could see where
the bullet had entered high on the hip. Thick black fur
was matted with dry blood. But the hole had apparently clotted as the wound no longer bled.

Travis could only see one entry hole. So why were both
legs useless? The bullet must have angled down from
one side to the other, he reasoned. That's probably why
it was running on three legs when he had first caught a
glimpse of it earlier. The slug must have stopped some-

where in the muscle of opposite leg. The limb had stiffened and had become too painful to use.

Holding the jacket in one hand, Travis extended the other and lightly stroked the animal's back. The wolf growled, and then sensing no harm, let its head fall back on its paws. Always talking, Travis continued the petting. The stroking and gentle voice seemed to make the animal relax. Its breathing slowed, and the rapid rise and fall of its rib cage lessened.

What now, Travis mused, continuing to caress and chat at the same time. What should he do about a wounded wolf—in the midst of a snow storm—in the middle of nowhere?

The youth knelt behind the yearling, uncertain what his next move should be. After a moment or two, he slowly stood upright, all the while thinking. The wolf lifted its head, twisted its neck, and with large, amber-colored eyes, stared at the teenager.

"Okay, okay, you win," Travis mumbled, "I'll see what I can do."

He retrieved the survival tool from deep within the bib's big pocket. A dense stand of young aspen sprouts grew nearby. Using the tool's longest blade, Travis began chopping at the thumb-sized trunk of the nearest tree. After giving the soft bark a half-dozen whacks, he stood, grabbed the sapling with both hands, and pulled toward the ground. The slender stalk snapped, breaking clean where the gashes had been made.

Travis continued hacking away with the knife, forming a plan as he worked. He didn't stop until a half-dozen saplings lay on top of the snow. Now he needed some way to lash the poles together.

Returning to the backpack, he pulled the sleeping bag from its pouch. Tugging the drawstring, he cut the knot off one end, and then pulled the cord free. The nylon string was thin, but strong, and, he hoped, long enough to do the job.

Facing the pup, Travis could see it hadn't made any attempt at escape. Except for its labored breathing, the wolf lay motionless. "Hang in there. Be patient. I'm doing the best I can," the boy whispered. "And if we're going to keep having these one-sided conversations, you'll need a name. With all that beautiful black fur, you're darker than a clothes closet in the middle of the night. Hey! That's it! I'm gonna call you Midnight. It's a perfect fit."

Travis began stomping snow. He needed a work place. When a small area had been packed, he was ready to start the building process. He had already cut the two thickest saplings into equal lengths. These he placed several feet apart on the ground.

The next chore was cutting other stalks into shorter sections. Once that was done, he placed one of the short pieces crossways over the longer pair. He wrapped the cord around where the sticks crossed, pulled tight, and tied it off. Satisfied the knot would hold, he cut the line.

He examined the remaining length of string. Nearly a foot had been used to make one connection. At that rate there wouldn't be enough of the tough cord to finish the job. It was probably best to save the nylon fiber for the four outside corners—use the poacher's twine on middle sections. When the tying material came to an end, six cross pieces were lashed tight to the parallel poles. Ready or not, having run out of string, the project was complete.

Travis took a moment to study the surroundings. Large feathery flakes still tumbled from the sky silently rounding off nature's angles, making hard things look soft and plush. The wolf hadn't moved. The animal was becoming part of the background. All but its eyes and nose sported a new white coat.

Shaking his head, Travis returned to reality. The plan was to use the sapling contraption as a sled: the poles on one end held off the ground, the other end dragging through the snow. The hard part would be putting the pup aboard, and then getting the animal to go along for the ride.

With parka in hand, Travis circled behind the yearling. He gently brushed a bit of snow from the wolf's fur, being careful to keep well away from the injured area. At the first touch, the animal turned its head, and for a moment, studied the teenager. Then it put its head down as if to say, 'do what you have to, I'm too tired to fight.'

Resuming his gentle monologue, Travis opened the jacket alongside the animal. He moved to the opposite side, making sure his glove was pulled up over his wrist. Then he knelt in the snow and started burrowing. "There ya go. There ya go. Easy now. Just wanna help you out here, pup."

Travis fully extended his arm, and then wiggled his fingers until he could grasp an edge of the coat. He tugged gently, pulling part of the parka under the animal. He repeated the process in several places. Only when the teen was burrowing near the injury did the wolf acknowledge the activity. It whimpered once, startling Travis, but made no attempt to bite.

It was time for the most difficult part of the plan. The tall teenager stopped talking and straddled the young predator. Throwing caution to the wind, Travis bent, bunched both sides of the jacket in his hands, and began lifting. Disturbed, and despite being injured, the pup tried to escape.

Travis had forgotten the first rule—continual chattering. "Whoa. It's all right. I'm not going to hurt you. Settle down, settle down." The words found their mark. As quickly as it begun, the protest was over. The young wolf went limp.

With the yearling resting on the drag, Travis was faced with another problem. The jacket had to be secured to the rig or the wolf-filled parka would slip off. He pulled out a stretch cord from the packframe bag. Acting as if the animal understood English, the youth babbled constantly, outlining the plan.

"Ya see, Midnight, first I'll tie the sleeves together around the top cross bar. I'll zip you in tight and use this rubber thingie at the bottom to keep you from falling off. Should work, don't cha think?"

After knotting the sleeves around the top bar, Travis made several short slits in the bottom edge of the jacket. Into these holes he threaded one end of the stretch cord. When that was completed, he pulled both ends of the cord until the bottom of the parka drew together like a laundry bag. Finished tying off the bungee, Travis stood quiet inspecting his work, wondering if the contraption would even hold together.

* * *

Seth stood in front of the lake front window, quietly watching flakes flinging themselves against the frost-covered glass. The mid-day forecast hadn't sounded anything like the prediction given the prior evening. An unexpected wind shift was the weatherman's excuse. As long as the wind kept coming over from Lake Superior, snow would continue to fall.

Restless, Seth checked the kitchen clock: twelve-twenty. In a couple of hours he'd have to leave to pick up Trav. He was concerned timing might be a problem as Travis' watch wasn't working. With the sun being yesterday's memory, Seth wondered if his buddy would arrive on schedule.

Anxious to do something, Seth went to the hall closet and started gathering up snowmobile gear. Visibility outside was low. The snowmobile ride would probably take longer than the day before. But first he'd make a sandwich, and afterwards, just to be safe, pack a few snacks. His buddy might be late—and he might be hungry.

* * *

Mrs. Larsen had an unsettled feeling. Even here, next to the warmer waters of Lake Superior, snow was falling from a low, leaden-colored sky. Thick wet flakes were sticking to the windowpane. If it was snowing in town, it was almost certain to be doing the same over the big hill.

She had phoned home over lunch break. Beth confirmed her concern. "Yeah, Mom. It's snowing so hard that when I look out the double doors, I can't even see the lake. It's been coming down since I got up. Looks like it'd be over my boots, but I'm not sure. I haven't gone outside yet."

Was history repeating itself? Would Travis have enough sense to head for home as soon as he saw the change in the weather? At least he has winter clothing, she reasoned, returning her gaze to the clipboard in her hands. He shouldn't be cold.

Chapter Six

C H A P T E R   S I X

He had already worked up a sweat. Pulling the rig was
a burdensome task. For the first few yards the yearling
objected, struggling to gain its freedom. But without
use of its rear legs, and weakened by the wound, the
animal didn't have the strength or energy to make
much of an effort. After several half-hearted attempts,
the pup put its muzzle down on its front paws and
went along for the ride.

Travis trudged wearily ahead, a pole end clutched
tightly in each hand. He kept up a steady chatter,
putting thoughts into words, as if the wolf could
comprehend. "Okay Midnight, here's the rest of the
program. When we get to the lake, I'll follow the shoreline and then hike to the landing. We'll decide what
to do next when we get there—stay put or head for
the highway."

When he was alone on the autumn adventure, Travis
often caught himself speaking out loud. It was one way
of keeping fear in check—of dealing with panic. He
was becoming more nervous by the minute. Plodding
through the white carpet was difficult. The drag was
painful to pull, each step was a strain. Instead of the rig
riding on top, as he had pictured, the rear poles cut

into the powder like skate blades—acting more like brakes than sled runners.

Had not a hazy wall of flakes fogged in the space between snow-laden trees, Travis might have seen the lake. It was nearby, not a hundred yards away. The course he was traveling angled much farther up the shoreline. The easterly heading was making the trip much longer than necessary.

A half-dozen rest stops later, Travis was treading downhill. Just ahead the trees opened up. With a few quick steps both he and the drag were resting on top of a steep bank. Below, looking like a flat, white rug, lay the snow covered surface of Mystery Lake.

The relief he felt was like a gentle spring breeze. No longer did he have to worry about becoming confused. All he had to do now was follow the shoreline. In spite of the whiteout, he would easily recognize the spruce grove. From there it was only a short walk to the main trail. If things went right, he would be back to the highway before dark. Seth would be waiting with the snowmobile. They'd both make it home in time for a late supper.

From his house he could call a warden, explain about leaving the wounded wolf at the landing. Even in the dark, rangers could use snowmobiles to make a rescue. Once they had the injured animal in the back of a pickup, they could rush it to a vet. Despite the poacher's devious plot, everything was going to work out.

The teen paused to check the yearling, make sure it was securely bundled in the jacket. He opened the hood slowly. The wolf lay motionless, its breathing fast, its eyes dull. "Hang in there, Midnight, everything's gonna to be all right," Travis whispered, giving the animal's lush fur a gentle brush of his hand.

Leaving the drag where it sat, Travis explored the top of the ridge, looking for the best approach to the lake.

He'd have to bring everything down in one trip. The slope was far too steep to climb back up. Fifty yards downshore a section of bluff had caved inward. The top portion was abrupt and formed a chute, but then the slope became more gradual as it neared the water.

Marching back to the rigging, Travis took a moment to enjoy half an energy bar. He stuck the other half in a pocket, burped loudly as if finishing a real meal, and concluded enough time had been wasted.

Sliding down the embankment was an athletic dare. After considering several possibilities, Travis chose to slide down on his rear. With legs extended out front, he placed the pack in his lap, pulled the drag poles past his middle, held tight, and headed downhill. Luckily for his rear-end, the soft snow slowed his descent. Bouncing on his bottom like a runaway bobsledder, he raced down the hill, towing the drag along for the ride.

Dazed, but not hurt, he rose, brushed snow from his bibs, and made a quick check of the passenger. The pup had made the trip without further injury. Eager to get home, Travis slipped into the pack harness, grasped the drag poles, and moved out onto the ice.

His first full step plunged him into a new predicament. The ice hadn't formed nearly thick enough to handle the snow load. Lake water had had already seeped up through cracks and breaks. Worse, except for the very top, the new snow had become a thick, wet mush. Slush would not only make walking difficult, it was dangerous. He would never know if the next step would be his last.

Terrified, he stopped in mid-step, took a deep breath, and began mumbling directions to himself. "Stay cool, stay cool. You'll find a way to solve this." Snowflakes were falling at a more moderate rate, and through the haze, Travis could make out the shoreline for several hundred yards ahead. For as far as he could see the steep-sided slope continued right to the lake's edge.

A quick study of the map verified this location was well past the bluff where he had wanted to fish. He shuddered recalling the thin ice and how easily the chisel had sliced through. That had been a scary close call. With new snow and tons of wet slush already straining the lake surface, he'd have to be crazy to travel close to the cliff face.

Why? Why couldn't things ever be easy? It seemed every time he planned a simple adventure, he was given a test. He should have just stayed home and fished in front of the house like his mom had suggested.

Like it or not, there was only one choice. Somehow he'd have to get back up the slope. Once on land, he could follow the heavily timbered ridge above the lake's edge. Traveling on the flat ice surface just wasn't an option. Travis turned to study the shoreline in the other direction. Except for far in the distance where spindly aspens poked up and out, the hill that direction was also too steep to climb.

Seeing no other alternative, Travis clutched up the drag poles. The skinny trees far down the shoreline were the best hope of getting off the ice. He could use them to help pull his way up the hill. In the meantime, he'd have to tread close to the steep-sided bank. What he couldn't do was stand gawking all day—there wasn't that much of the day left. He had to find a way up and off or he'd be spending the night on the lake.

Progress was much slower than Travis could have imagined. It took all his muscle power to pull the rig. If he relaxed his grip, the poles would slip from his grasp. Hands soon began cramping from the effort, and every few minutes the drag would have to be set down in order to wiggle his fingers. Equally annoying, icy slush clung to his footwear, turning his boots into a pair of concrete blocks. Every step forward was a muscle-testing ordeal.

What should have been a ten-minute hike used the better part of an hour. Before he dared move forward, Travis would test the ice. As if doing a slow-motion dance step, he would transfer weight cautiously to the forward foot. Then he would stand statue-like for a second or two before lifting his rear foot. Moaning like a troll under a bridge, the ice would occasionally groan out a warning. To Travis it sounded like it was telling him to keep off—to go away.

Perspiration mixed with melted flakes and ran into the corners of his eyes, blinding him. Every few strides he had to remove a glove and wipe away the moisture. What he could see was frightening. The land along shore dropped into the lake at a very steep angle. If the ice should give way, he'd be lucky to have time and space to flop against the slope—and save himself from drowning.

After much hard work, Travis reached the area of spindly trees. Like a boxer between rounds, he paused, hands on hips, gasping for breath. When his pulse slowed, and his breathing became more regular, his stomach growled, reminding him it hadn't been tended to. Reluctantly, he pulled the partially eaten bar from his pocket. He nibbled at it, savoring each tiny bite until he was holding only an empty wrapper. It was time to climb.

Looking a little like race poles on a ski hill, a half-dozen skinny aspen sprouts were spaced along the steep grade. Travis needed to bring everything up in one trip like he'd accomplished coming down. To do that, he'd have to plop on his back, dig his feet into the snow, push with his legs, and somehow pull the drag along as he went.

He made a quick check on the wolf. The animal's eyes were closed, but the rise and fall of its chest told him it was alive. "Hang in there, Midnight," Travis said softly. "We'll find a way out of this mess."

The drag was just long enough for the packframe to be strapped behind the parka. With everything secure, Travis started up the steep grade. The first few feet went easy. The rest of the ascent was much more difficult. He had needed the trees. Several times Travis had to brace a foot on a spindly trunk to keep everything from sliding back down the hill.

It took ten minutes of intensive effort before boy and wolf reached the summit. Once the rig was safe, Travis flopped in the snow, chest heaving and mouth open, sucking air. For the time being his energy was spent, and he lay flat with eyes shut—resting. But dressed only in shirt and vest, he soon became chilled. He became a bit alarmed when he sat up and discovered he was a snowman—coated from head to foot in white.

As Travis stood brushing off snow, a silent alarm rang in his head. He gazed out over the lake. Snowflakes were no longer tumbling straight down. The wind had picked up, pushing flakes slightly sideways. And he wasn't certain, maybe because he was damp, but it seemed that the temperature was dropping.

"Okay, okay, Ma Nature," he mumbled, "just keep your cool. We're out of here."

After slipping into the backpack harness, Travis clutched up the ends of the drag, and started off in the direction he had just come. The only good news was now that he was on land, he didn't have to worry about falling through thin ice.

* * *

61

Finished with gassing the snowmobile, Seth returned the half-full fuel container to the corner of the shed. It wasn't quite two o'clock, but he thought with such wintry conditions, Travis would have probably packed up early. He'd have wanted to be back to the blacktop long before dark.

Seth hadn't told anyone about the food packets. Grownups could sometimes make such a big deal about little things. Seth figured if Travis was hungry, his buddy could have seconds at the supper table. And just to make sure Trav wasn't too upset, Seth had stuffed a pocket with two Snickers bars and a bag of trail mix. He reasoned that those treats would be more than adequate to tide Travis over until they got back home.

He was about to open the large shed door when Rollie Kane suddenly popped through the side entrance. Rollie and his wife were owners of the resort. Seth thought they were about the nicest people he'd ever met. After the accidental death of Seth's father, it was the Kanes who had insisted the Springwoods move in at the lakeside retreat and help operate the long-established 'get-away.'

Rollie had encouraged Seth to travel along with summer canoe groups, to be an extra set of hands and eyes for resort guides as they portaged and paddled through the roadless area. By helping on trips, and listening to Rollie's suggestions, Seth had learned a great deal about the wilderness.

Rollie had become Seth's father, grandfather, and teacher, all in one gentle package. The elderly man had a special way about him. Always turning a blind eye to Seth's shortcomings, the kindly old fellow gave advice and direction without ever being bossy or critical.

"Going out for a ride on the big machine?" Rollie asked, thumping snow from his boots. "How's it running? That tune-up do any good?"

"Working great, Rollie. Runs like a fine Swiss watch," Seth replied with a grin.

Seth couldn't help but think how much Rollie reminded him of Santa Claus. With his portly middle, gray hair, and white beard, Rollie would make a perfect shopping mall Kris Kringle. The only thing missing, Seth thought, was a red suit and tall black boots.

"Seth, you know I don't want to tell ya what to do, but I'd be real nervous if you went running around on the lake today. All this wet snow has had to put an awful strain on the ice. Probably some slush out there you won't be able to see. That machine's pretty heavy. Don't know if one person could lift it free if it gets stuck."

"Oh, right. I'm not heading out on the ice. I'm gonna follow the shoreline to the other end of the lake and pick up the snowmobile trail. Yesterday I dropped Trav off at the trailhead to Mystery Lake. He was gonna hike back and do some walleye fishing."

"Well, I hope he had good luck. A fresh fried walleye fillet would taste mighty good this time of year. Maybe tomorrow you and I should try to catch something, That is if you don't mind an old man standing out on the ice with you."

"Rollie, you're not an old man. You're a better fisherman than I'll ever be. Yeah, if it's not windy, let's do it. We can use the snowmobile to tow the gear along the beach to the point. We can walk out a ways from there."

"Great. Looking forward to it. I'll tell Kate not to thaw anything out for supper tomorrow night. I'm going to say you promised us fresh fish for dinner. How's that for putting the ball in your court?" Rollie smiled, showing off his store-bought teeth.

"You're on. Fresh fish it is. Right now I better get going. I'm suppose to meet Trav at three. With the way it's coming down, I'll have to take it slow on the trail. Visibility won't be all that great."

"You go ahead, sounds like a fun ride. If I wasn't so stiff, I'd take the small machine and ride along with you. Start 'er up. I'll get the door."

Seth pulled on his helmet, cranked the engine, and idled out of the building. Once outside, he fed the machine gas and roared off. Rollie was left standing in a haze of blue smoke, wishing he were at least ten years younger. He loved traveling in and about the Boundary Waters Canoe Area, but at his age he found it easier to get somewhere if his transportation had a steering wheel and four big tires. Except for the main highway and a few side trails, most of the BWCAW was off-limits to him: things with motors and wheels were illegal in the wilderness area.

* * *

It was a struggle, but Travis finally reached the top of the cliff-faced rise. Resting on one knee, peering out over the lake, a razor-edged wind cut at his nose and cheeks. Below, on the flat surface, wind gusts chased eddies of loose powder. Where the white swirls touched shore, they tired of the game—called a recess—and huddled in small waves along the wood-line.

The trek along the ridge had been both time-consuming and difficult. He often had to detour into the forest to avoid clumps of windfalls. Shouldering the packframe, while pulling the drag, took an enormous effort. The climb to the bluff top had been exhausting. Muscles and joints were crying for relief, begging for rest.

Travis questioned if he had the energy to go on. Most of the day had already been spent. In a few hours it'd be dark. The conflict was: should he set up camp now or continue plodding toward home?

He relaxed a few minutes, resting, then stood and shuffled along the bluff for a better view. Down the opposite slope he could see the evergreens—the spot where this nightmarish ordeal had its origin. Travis made his decision. He'd pull the drag to the spruce grove, pitch the tent, and search for the fish fillet that had been tossed over the trees. He would get a good night's sleep and head for home in the morning.

Tonight, when he didn't show up at the trailhead, Seth would call his folks. They'd no doubt call the sheriff's office. A Search and Rescue team would be out at first light looking for him. It'd be a long night for his mom, but she'd be okay with it after he told her the reason why it wasn't his fault he couldn't stick to the schedule.

Going down was much easier than going up. Travis didn't pause until he reached the evergreens. And as it turned out, the stop was a wise choice. Just ahead the needled trees were tightly spaced. Snow-covered boughs hung close to the ground, creating a barrier of green and white. He needed to find a route to the camp opening without bringing tons of snow down on his head. He'd just finished checking the wolf. The yearling seemed to be sleeping so Travis kept quiet. There was no need to disturb its rest.

Human speech suddenly broke the quiet, halting Travis in his tracks. The panic he'd been holding in rose in his throat, almost gagging him. He immediately knew who was talking. If he lived to be a hundred, he'd never forget that voice. The sound was that unusual, almost as if the man had eaten breakfast at a gravel bar or swallowed steel wool. The voice belonged to the tall wolf killer. But why were they still in the area? The answer came quickly from the man who had tied Travis to the tree.

"I'm gettin' fed up with all your whining. I think I shoulda left you in the woods instead of that punk kid.

We ain't gonna get caught. Only one person knows and he ain't gonna be doin' any talking."

"I'm tellin' ya, Frank, you're nuttier than a squirrel's nest. Stop and think about it. Soon as that kid turns up missing, these woods will be full of lawmen. It ain't like he's some homeless orphan. Teenager out here with all that fancy gear has to have a family waitin' on him. When he doesn't show up at home, a whole posse of people will be out huntin' for him."

"Well now, that's the joy of it. If somebody should happen to see us, all we gotta say is we saw the boy yesterday. That he was way up the trail, truckin' along in the other direction. They'll move the search site. With all the commotion, we'll ski out without anyone the wiser."

There was a break in the conversation, and for a moment, the world went quiet. Travis was sure the men could hear his heart pounding up against his ribs. He held his breath and strained his ears.

The portly man's squeaky voice filled the air. "You are one-hundred-percent insane! What if the kid makes it out alive? What if they find him? He can identify us, Frank, didn't ya think of that?"

"Yeah, I did. First of all, I doubt very much the kid'll ever be found. Come spring, he'll be crow food. And even if they find him alive, so what?"

This was even worse than the morning scare. Travis now knew just how ruthless the tall wolf killer could be.

"So what?" Squeaky voice shrieked. "So what if the kid tells about a dead wolf and the fur coat we stole off its back? How we gonna explain that?"

"You know what, Rusty? You worry too much. You want to leave, do it. Just remember it was your idea to come back and look for the kid in the first place. If ya weren't such a yellow-bellied jellyfish, we'd be long gone."

"Yeah, well that's 'cause I thought we might find him. I don't wanna be lookin' at no murder rap. I thought maybe we could reason with the kid. Tell him it was only a test. Tell him that if he ever talked, we'd sneak back some day and do him for real."

"But we didn't find him. Did we? You know why? 'Cause he's lost, and without fire and food, he'll be lucky to make it through the night."

"That's where your wrong, Frank. That ain't no city kid. Tell me, what kind of a boy goes out in the boonies in the first place? I'll tell you what kind. It's a kid that grew up in the woods just like we did. Think about it. He probably knows as much about handlin' himself out here as we do."

Gravel voice rudely interrupted. "Oh, get serious. That kid can't be more than fourteen or fifteen. How much could he know?"

"Plenty. And don't forget, you left him with his tent and sleeping bag. It ain't like he's dressed in party clothes. Besides, its not all that cold. He ain't gonna freeze tonight."

"Well, I ain't gonna freeze either. Set up the tents and get a fire started. I'll put the gun back together and sit near the lake. Who knows, with the wind blowing my scent into the woods, maybe I'll get lucky and get us another fur coat. Give a shout when you've got some-thin' ready to eat."

Travis realized this was worse than bad news. This was a disaster. The poachers were planning on camping in his spot overnight. Now he was trapped. He didn't dare try sneaking along the lake. If the tall dude spotted him, it'd be all over. Somehow he'd have to double back and go around the evergreen grove.

Dropping to his knees, Travis began crawling, turning the drag with him as he quietly clambered to get away. His hand struck something hard and smooth. A bit of luck—it was the plastic sack containing the fish fillet. He quickly scooped the package from the snow and slid it into the large pouch pocket of his bibs. At least he'd have something to eat tonight, but he couldn't think about that now. First he had to make his getaway. Dead boys don't need food.

When Travis put enough distance between himself and the poachers to feel safe, he stopped, stood, and brushed snow from his clothing. His shirt sleeves were wet. They'd have to be dried next to a fire, but that would have to come later. What he needed now was a new strategy. He pulled the chart from his pocket, studied it, and mulled over his options. With his finger he found the lake and the line representing the trail.

Somehow he would have to circle around the poachers' camp and head cross country. Another thought occurred to him. Using the trail still might be risky. 'Thick' and 'Thin,' as Travis pictured the unusual two-some, would be using the trail in the morning.

He stared off in space, pondering that possibility. Maybe it'd be best to keep to the woods, forget about using the path altogether. Right now he had to put some space between himself and the two characters who had caused all his problems.

According to the map, he'd need to head southwest. Travis took a quick compass reading, then looked ahead to pick a target. Cloaked in winter white, every-thing in the forest looked much the same. Off in the distance, through falling snow, he spotted a towering Norway pine. The stately tree was to the right of his preferred course, but it would have to do. He would use that as his first rest stop.

Travis checked on the wolf before starting off. Since his close encounter with the poachers, he'd almost forgotten why he was pulling the drag. The pup was alive, but its breathing seemed labored. All the sleeping can't be a good sign, Travis concluded. This was a wild animal, and though it was young, it should be trying to escape. Sleeping would be the last thing it would do.

"Hang in there, Midnight," he whispered. "We'll get through this together."

Taking a moment to reclaim his target tree, Travis grabbed up a drag pole in each hand and started plodding toward the large evergreen.

Chapter Seven

C H A P T E R   S E V E N

Daylight, already stained gray by a concrete-colored sky and snow-filled air, was fading fast. Night would drop like a stage curtain. Progress through the forest had been agonizingly slow. Towing the drag was a muscle-testing ordeal, almost an overload. Even without the parka, Travis was perspiring, and had to stop often to catch his breath, cool down. Every fiber and nerve pleaded for a timeout. Thirst and hunger added to his misery—he was literally dog tired. Trudging over a rise, Travis knew he was done for the day. Like coins at a carnival, his energy was spent.

Ahead, dozens of trees had been tossed about like a spoiled child's discarded toys. A finger of wind from the autumn storm had obviously dropped down to nick this part of the forest. Even if he had the strength, there was no way could he hike through the maze in the dark. The only choice was to make camp, continue on in the morning.

To his right, nestled in the snow as if it were napping, lay the top of a huge spruce. Its needled boughs made a windbreak—a good place to pitch the tent. The tired teen barely had strength to pack snow before attempting to set up the shelter. All he wanted to do was unroll his sleeping bag—crawl in—go to sleep. That wasn't going to happen just yet. There were camp chores to finish before thinking about bed.

When the tent was up, the bag ready, Travis began gathering fuel. A birch blowdown provided paper-like bark for the tinder nest. With a pocket full of shreddings, the weary youth went about breaking branches from nearby windfalls.

These he dragged to the tent area. Travis knew fire could be a hungry friend. If you wanted to share its warmth and light, you had to feed it often. In the time it took to collect enough wood to make a meager pile, dusk had settled over the forest.

Travis needed a place for fire and began kicking snow. When a small area had been tramped, he positioned the tinder, added twigs, and then removed the back cover of the compass, exposing a strip of gray material. With everything ready, he reached into his bibs and pulled out the survival tool.

Kneeling next to the fire nest, Travis pulled a stubby little blade across the drab-colored strip of flint. Like tiny fireworks, a burst of yellowish red sparks flew off, several landing on the shreddings. Without a moment's delay, Travis crouched close and puffed. A thin wisp of smoke rose and tickled his nostrils. He blew again, causing the tinder to come alive with fire.

At first, only a few modest flames nibbled at the shredding. With another lungful of air, the fire started feeding on sticks and branches. Travis carefully added larger pieces of wood. Success—he had fire. He could dry clothes, cook the fish, and melt snow to fill the water bottle. Most important, he wouldn't freeze.

Preoccupied with camp chores, the boy had neglected the wolf. The pulling contraption, with its pup-filled parka, lay alongside the spruce boughs. Before thawing the fish fillet, Travis thought best he check on the animal. He trudged to the drag, propped the flashlight in the snow, and unzipped the jacket.

Surprise was seeing the yearling staring back, its eyes wide with fear and caution. A low growl came from deep in the young predator's throat, warning Travis to keep hands off. "Okay, okay, I won't bother you. Just glad to see you're still with us," Travis said in a gentle tone. "Maybe you'll feel different about things when I have supper ready."

Travis used the longest knife blade to chop the fillet into two pieces. He returned one piece to the bag; put the other in the pot. Around the fillet he packed snow. His plan was to make fish soup. Tired muscles and joints needed fluids as much as food.

Using a simple tripod made from branches, Travis dangled the hinged-handled pot over the fire. When the first snow melted, he added more of the powdered water. It was almost an hour before the pot was filled with liquid and began to steam. All the while Travis had poked and prodded the fish meat, fracturing the light flesh into smaller and smaller pieces.

Finally, when almost a third of the water had steamed into space, Travis removed the pot from the flames. He set it aside, waited a few moments, and then sampled its contents. Delicious, mighty delicious, he thought, taking another sip. He had just taught himself another way to fix fish.

Travis slowly sipped his supper. The pot was nearly empty before he remembered that the pup, too, had gone all day without food or drink. Struggling to stand, he rekindled the fire, put more snow in the pot, and hung it back over the flames.

Having something in his belly, and feeling better, the youth stayed close to the blaze, savoring its heat, while new snow melted and mixed with a bit of leftover broth. When the snow melt had warmed to the touch, he pulled the drag closer to the flames. He stroked the jacket fabric, continually talking. "Midnight, here's the deal. You need to eat and drink just like me. I'm willing to share some of my supper if you promise not to chew my hand off."

With the parka partly open, and the pup straining to free itself, the boy babbled on. "Look, I know you're in no condition to go anywhere. You're gonna have to stay with me, at least 'til you're feeling better. You'll starve to death on your own."

Travis pulled a waterproof mitten onto his left hand. He cupped the palm face up, poured a small pool of weak soup into the depression, and slowly brought the mitten below the pup's muzzle. With firelight reflecting in its eyes, the cautious predator studied the human, trying to make sense of the offering. After a long moment, and from between dagger-like canine teeth, a pink-tinted tongue poked out to lap up the liquid. The action was repeated over and over until the pot was empty.

Travis set the pan in the snow and stood. "Wolf, it's time for bed. You, my friend, can sleep under the stars, not that any are out tonight. And don't even think of leaving. We'll have another go at fish soup in the morning."

After zipping the jacket, and pulling the drag under the evergreen boughs, the tired trekker was more than ready to call it a day. Away from the fire he could tell the temperature had continued to fall. There wasn't a thing he could do about it. All he could do was bundle into his bag and hope that sometime soon the snow would end.

* * *

Seth had remembered to wear his watch. He pulled up at the trailhead a few minutes early. He stretched, plunked himself on the padded seat, and waited patiently for Travis to come plodding up the trail. Actually, the ride had been fun. His was the first snowmobile to travel over the fresh matting. The teen marveled at how easily the long-tracked machine climbed hills and hugged curves as it ate up miles.

The first half hour flashed by. Seth had at first been excited and warmed by the trip. But when four o'clock had come and gone, concern grew to worry. Sun or no sun, Trav would have headed for home during the middle part of the day. And if that was the case, why hadn't he shown up yet?

All afternoon plump flakes had somersaulted and tumbled as they skydived to earth from overhead swirls of gray—at times dancing sideways, pushed by sudden puffs of wind. It would be dark soon. With such heavy cloud cover, Seth knew there'd be no twilight. And except for the occasional hum of a car rushing by on the blacktop, the forest remained secretive and silent.

The longer Seth sat, the more he shivered. It was one thing to ride and play—that was work and kept him warm. It was different to just sit and wait. As dusk darkened the forest, the teen stood and began stomping around the snowmobile. A decision had to be made. Should he continue to wait, or should he head for help?

He was about to pull the starter cord when the sweep of headlights cut through the haze. A vehicle had pulled into the parking area. A door slammed. Someone was calling his name. At first Seth didn't recognize the voice. When he realized who it was, he hollered back. "Over here! I'm parked on the edge of the trail."

"Stay there," the voice urged. "I'll come to you." Moments later the broad shouldered outline of Mr. Larsen appeared. "Seth, glad you didn't leave. Any sign of Trav?"

"Nothing, Mr. Larsen. Jeez, I'm sure glad to see you. But I thought you were out of town on business."

"I was," the man answered, stopping alongside the Polaris. "Just got home a little while ago. I hopped in the car when I heard Trav wasn't back yet. What time were you supposed to meet him?"

"We agreed on three o'clock. But just before he took off, he discovered that the battery in his watch went dead. I'm thinking he lost track of time," Seth said, tugging up a sleeve to check his watch.

"Let's hope that's all that's lost. Do you know where he was planning to camp?"

Seth hesitated. He thought Travis would had specified the exact camping spot with his parents. "Not exactly. Just somewhere near Mystery Lake."

Roger studied the trail entrance for a second or two as if expecting to see Travis appear at any moment. "You must be an ice cube from sitting so long. Why don't you return to the resort? When you get home, call Linda. Tell her I'm going to stay and wait for Trav. If I'm not home by seven, have her call the sheriff's office. Tell her to send a deputy up here."

"Thanks. I am chilled," Seth stammered through chattering teeth. "I'll call soon as I get back. Do ya think somebody should start looking for Trav tonight or will they wait 'til morning?"

"Probably both. Let's hope he's here soon. Go ahead, start the snowmobile. I'll go wait in the wagon. If I leave the engine running, I can keep the lights on. I'm sure Travis will know they're for him."

* * *

Roger looked at his watch for the third time in the past fifteen minutes. Seven-thirty and still no sign of his son.

Suddenly an extra set of headlights joined his own—bright beams slashing a white gash through a flake-filled backdrop.

The thud of a car door closing was followed by a rap at the passenger window. Roger reached across and pulled the door handle open. "Evening," came a man's voice. "Mind if I have a seat?"

"No, come in. I've been expecting you," Roger replied through the cold of the open door.

"Caught the call about ten miles down the Gunflint. Want to fill me in?" the officer requested, notepad in hand.

"Not a whole lot to tell. My son was dropped off here early yesterday morning. He was planning to hike the trail, do some fishing, be back here by three today."

"Let me guess," the deputy said. "This the same kid who spent a couple of weeks in the woods after the big blowdown storm?"

"Yeah, it is. With the weather so mild, his mother and I saw no problem with a solo overnight. There was no mention of snow in the forecast. Right now I'm worried he might have fallen through the ice."

"As I recall, you folks live down on Poplar Lake. Your boy must have lots of experience with lake ice," the deputy said, jotting something in the notebook.

"Well...that's true. Except this year, with all the warm weather, who knows how thick the ice is under the snow? Might be a foot in one place, only an inch or two a few feet away."

"Tell you what," the deputy said, closing the notepad and turning to look at Mr. Larsen. "There's not a whole lot we can do right now. A little too dark and snowy to start a full-blown rescue effort. But, just to be safe, we'll ask someone from the ranger station to run up and down the trail on a snowmobile. Who knows, maybe that's all we'll need to do. Maybe your boy got pooped and stopped for the night."

The man paused, considering the situation before continuing. "In the meantime, I'll notify Search and Rescue. For sure they'll want to have a better look in the morning. I'd bet they'll let you join them. You have access to a snowmobile?"

Roger thought about that for a moment. "Trav's buddy was waiting here with a two-seater. I'm sure he'd want to help. I can probably ride along with him. The only place we could drive, though, would be on the trail. We wouldn't dare head out on the lake."

"Yep. You're right about that. But, Mr. Larsen, have you heard the latest forecast? I'm afraid it's not promising for an air search. They're saying an Alberta Low is sliding down from Canada. Suppose to arrive overnight."

"Major storm! What's that falling in our headlights?"

"The weather people say that's still lake effect snow. When this next system moves in, it could snow steady for two or three days. Maybe some wind and cold temps, too. I sure hope your boy brought along extra grub. He may be stuck back there for a few days."

Chapter Eight

Sometime during the long, dark hours of night the snow tapered off. In the morning only an inch or two of overnight fluff lay on top the tent. The evening before, when Travis had slipped into the winter bag, he thought he'd have trouble falling asleep. That wasn't the case. Despite his worries, and his memories of the autumn storm, within minutes he was sawing wood. The long, hard day had completely worn him down. His body demanded rest. Travis slept without waking until nearly dawn.

Slipping into bibs and boots, he took care of his needs, and then checked on his camping companion. Inside the parka the pup was curled in a ball. The young wolf lifted its head and stared at Travis. Only this time, unlike the night before, it didn't growl.

After giving the animal a friendly greeting, the teen tended to camp work. He was hoping to find a hot coal to rekindle the fire. No such luck—only cold ashes. The blaze had to be rekindled using the flint. More than an hour passed before the soup was ready. And as he did the night before, Travis shared the last bit of broth. This time the wolf didn't hesitate. It quickly lapped up the offering.

Another half hour passed thawing snow to fill the water bottle. The morning was cold—well below freezing. Once the container was full, Travis slipped it into the big bib pouch. There body heat would keep it from becoming an ice block.

Anxious to be on his way, he'd rolled up the bag and tent while snow was melting in the pot. After securing both to the packframe, he took another look at the snowshoes. Both outer frames had been split, making the shoes useless. They'd have to be fixed in shop class. Right now he was fortunate the snow was only a foot or so deep. Any more than that and hiking would nearly be impossible.

He thought about the drag. The makeshift contraption had been so difficult to pull. If only he'd brought along a lightweight plastic snow-boat. A sled would ride on top of the snow. It'd be so much easier to tug.

Off in the blowdowns, Travis spotted the top of a giant pine. Before breaking completely free, the shattered end had split into several board-like pieces. One section looked thin and wide, and for a moment, Travis pondered its possibilities. If the thin section could be snapped off, he might be able to make a toboggan. The work would take time, but the results should be well worth the effort.

Postponing departure, he trudged over to the enormous tree top. Needle-laden boughs held the broken section far off the ground so he had to use a limb as a ladder. By holding on to branches to steady himself, Travis pushed snow aside with his boots as he shuffled his way to the tattered end. Once there, he stepped down on a thick finger of splintered wood.

Grasping the thin section in both hands, Travis lifted with all his strength. Nothing moved. He steadied himself, all the while thinking. The survival tool might be up to the task. The wood could be scored where he wanted the break.

Determined the idea would work, Travis drew the tip of the knife across the uneven wooden surface. He repeated the action again and again until the scratch became a groove. Ten minutes passed and he was ready to try lifting again. Still nothing. The board didn't budge. The cut would have to be deeper yet.

One slash at a time, the groove became a small valley. Travis was ready to make another attempt at breaking the board free. Setting the survival tool farther up the trunk, he prepared for the lift. He bent at the knees, gave a grunt, and pulled up with all his strength.

Sounding like a rifle shot, and as if it had been hit by a truck, the plank suddenly snapped. Taken by surprise, Travis was thrown off balance. It was already too late to save himself from falling. Looking like a big clumsy bird, the teen toppled from the log, arms wind-milling in thin air.

His right foot had slipped free of the pine tree perch. The left foot wasn't as fortunate. The boot became wedged between layers of splintered wood. Worse, the trapped leg was bent at an odd angle, sending a searing pain through his knee. Even before striking the ground, Travis knew the rules of escape had changed.

The unexpected fall whooshed his breath away and he lay in the snow with eyes shut tight, waiting to recover. When he could breathe again, he wiped snow from his face and tried to sit up. A paralyzing ache surged through the injured limb. Trying to will away the agony, Travis rolled his head back and let out a few short bursts of air that swirled up like smoke signals. Now, much like the temperature, the odds of hiking out on his own had just gone down.

Despite the hurt, Travis knew he had to move or his core temperature would drop. Getting back to the fire was top priority. But first he wanted to retrieve the tool. He discovered, that as long as the knee was bent, the ache was becoming tolerable. The problem would be reaching up to the splintered end of the tree top.

The plank-slab lay nearby atop the snow. Using the board as a wide crutch, Travis hobbled alongside the windfall. He grabbed the stub of a broken bough for support and stood tall on one leg, searching with his free hand. It remained empty.

He swallowed panic, tried a second time. Still nothing. A shudder coursed through every fiber, muscle, and nerve. Without the tool, he couldn't make fire. And without fire, he couldn't send up a smoke signal. And worse—much worse—he couldn't keep the cold away.

After a moment of indecision, and not knowing what else to do, Travis began muttering out loud. "Don't panic. Don't panic. Keep calm. The tool's here someplace. It didn't fly away. You'll find it. You just haven't looked in the right spot."

He sucked in a big breath, shook his head, and continued the one sided conversation. "Okay, decide what to do first. You know it's here. It probably fell into the snow when the board snapped. You'll find it later. First thing is to get back to the fire. Make sure it doesn't go out. Now step two. Think how to do that on one leg."

He was leaning on the solution—the pine plank. The top of the tree had bent before breaking free of the lower trunk. Before it had snapped completely off, the end of the splintered section had twisted itself into a ski-like curve. The board would slide over the snow like a toboggan. Determined to reach the fire, Travis plunked the board flat, lowered onto his good knee, and sat, backwards. With the good leg providing power, he began pushing himself to camp.

A small satisfaction was having stockpiled a fuel supply. Enough tinder remained to keep a small blaze burning for a few more hours. Maybe by then the knee would feel better. What he needed to do next was unfold the shelter near the fire. He could crawl in the sleeping bag and lie on the tent fabric—maybe even pull some of the fabric over the bag to help stay dry and warm while the leg rested.

Though it was a painful undertaking, Travis managed to open the tent and lay the material flat. He unrolled the sleeping bag, and using it like a quilt, pulled the warm covering over his body. Then he settled in, hoping the throbbing would ease. He was about to close his eyes when he noticed the wolf moving about in the parka.

Travis reluctantly left the bag, rolled onto the plank, and pushed until he was alongside the drag. Then, after removing a glove, he pulled the zipper open. The pup stopped struggling, surprised at suddenly being exposed. "Glad to see you're feeling better," Travis murmured. "Wish I could say the same."

The animal remained quite still, its body tense, eyes wide. About all Travis could do was stare back, wondering what the wolf was thinking. After a moment or two, he broke the spell. "Sorry, don't have anything to eat. We ate the fish for breakfast."

At the sound of boy's voice, the wolf tried desperately to stand. It rose on front legs, but rear legs refused to follow. The yearling whimpered, looked pleadingly at Travis, and eased back to its belly.

"I know how you must feel," Travis said softly. "We're two of a kind. I've got a similar problem. We're gonna have to stay put until I can figure a way out of this mess."

Returning to the blaze, Travis added a few sticks, then crawled under the covers. Flat on his back, he gazed vacantly up at the sky and mulled over his predicament. If the wind would calm, and the clouds cleared, he would add fuel to the fire. Family and friends had to be looking for him. When they didn't find him at the lake, there'd be an air search. Somebody would spot the smoke, radio his position to searchers, and he'd be rescued.

The difficult task would be gathering enough wood. With the injury, he would no longer be able to break branches by stomping on them. He'd probably need the knife to score limbs before snapping them into fuel-sized sections.

Travis repeated the plan in his head: find the knife—cut and break branches—listen for an airplane—stoke the fire—wait for a rescue. But first, he needed the parka. The morning air was too cold to go slowly rummaging about without wearing a warm coat.

The animal wasn't happy with the exchange. Travis had removed his vest and hobbled to the drag. But when he tried to coax the pup off the parka, it growled, showing teeth. The teen jerked his hand away from the wolf's muzzle. "Whoops, I forgot," he muttered. "You need to be talked into things."

Going painfully on all fours, Travis crawled to the animal's backside. "Okay, here's what we're gonna do. I need to get you off the jacket. You don't even need my coat. The one you were born with keeps you warm enough."

The teen cautiously reached out and touched the wolf on the back. Seeing no resistance, he started stroking the thick, black fur—all the time speaking in soothing tones. As the pup began to relax, Travis slowly worked his free hand under the wolf's middle. He continued the chatter while gently tugging at the parka. "Okay, here comes the touchy part," the boy whispered. "I hope you're not gonna bite my hand off."

Travis slipped both hands underneath the animal, lifted with his arms, and placed the pup on the open vest. The wolf gave a surprised yip but made no attempt to snap or bite. "That's about it, Midnight. That's all we're gonna do for now," the boy murmured, struggling to rise. Once upright, he slipped into the bright yellow jacket and limped back to the fire.

After adding fuel, Travis took a moment to warm his hands, and then headed for the pine. Using a birch branch for a crutch, each hobbled step sent a throbbing ache up and down his leg. The pain was almost more than he could bear, but he didn't stop. He had to find the tool.

Reaching the windfall, Travis leaned against a limb, resting. He couldn't ever remember hurting so bad. This injury was far worse than the portage trip accident. The canoe had fallen on his shoulder, cracking a collarbone. That bone wasn't a moving joint, hadn't kept him from hiking. Unless the knee made a miraculous recovery, he wouldn't be trekking very far anytime soon.

Yet, in the back corner of his mind, Travis knew he'd been lucky. The fall could have been disastrous. His leg could have snapped, and that hadn't happened. Looking up, he saw a bit of good news—the snow seemed to be easing off. Later, when the clouds lifted, he would feed the fire with green wood. By air or by land, somebody was sure to see the smoke.

* * *

Just before sunrise a small search group assembled at the trailhead. Because it was still uncertain Travis was in any real danger, an all-out rescue operation was put temporarily on hold. First a few snowmobilers would scour the trail and surrounding area, hoping to either locate the teen or find clues to his whereabouts.

Roger Larsen would ride behind Seth on the Polaris. The previous evening Rollie had helped Seth load the machine on a trailer. Then earlier that morning, Roger had hooked the rig to the Suburban so the three could ride together to the drop-off site. There they'd be joined by two other machines. One snowmobile would be driven by a ranger, the second by a warden.

Rollie hunkered in the SUV, eyeing the others readying for the ride. The elderly resort keeper had an uneasy feeling. He was well aware that lake ice couldn't be trusted this winter. Besides inadequate ice, the man was disturbed by the forecast. More snow was on its way. Only this time, along with the snow, the temperature would drop, escorted by a strong north wind. If Travis wasn't found first thing today, the boy could be in real trouble. The old man's thoughts were interrupted by the growl of snowmobile engines. He wiped a gloved hand across fogged-over window glass and watched as the machines disappeared into the woods.

What had taken Travis hours to hike, took only a fraction with snowmobiles. Not a sign of the boy had been seen. The only other tracks had been made by a single rider sent in to have a nighttime look. The forest was just waking to full light when the search party pulled up at the landing.

"What do you think?" Mr. Larsen inquired after they had tramped to the shoreline. "See any sign Trav camped here?"

"Pretty hard to tell with all the new snow," Warden Ambroy replied, pulling a red handkerchief from a rear pocket and wiping at his nose. "He certainly didn't camp at this landing last night."

"Say? Do you men smell smoke?" Seth asked, removing his helmet and sniffing at the air like a bloodhound.

"Yeah, now that you mention it, I do," the ranger agreed. "Look, down the lake a ways. Just before that bluff. Is that a wisp of gray rising out of that spruce grove?"

"I see it!" Mr. Larsen exclaimed. "Thank God! That's gotta be Trav. Who else would be back here this morning?"

"I think it would be safe for me to drive the snowmobile right next to shore," Seth volunteered. "That is, if it's all right with you," he added, looking at the wildlife officers.

"Hmm...it's highly irregular to allow machines on these wilderness lakes," the ranger said. "But considering the circumstances, go for it. You weigh less than the rest of us and would have the best chance of staying on top the slush. Just make sure you stay close to land as possible. It's not that far. We'll follow through the woods on foot."

Seth pulled on his helmet and ran to the Polaris. The three adults began hiking along the forested shoreline. Moments later they watched as Seth drove by, carefully keeping to the lake's edge.

The warden turned to Roger Larsen and grinned. "Looks like your boy just can't get enough of the woods. Maybe yesterday's snow spooked him. He probably chose to let it stop before heading home. For a while there it was really coming down."

"Maybe," Roger answered. "But I can't imagine him being hesitant to hike in snow. He was hoping to try out his new snowshoes and was even wishing for more of the white stuff."

"Well, there's your answer," the ranger added. "He probably stayed over hoping the snow would keep piling up. It'd give him an excuse to use his new equipment."

"Naw, I don't think so. It's not like Trav to do something like that. He knows how worried his mother gets when he's out by himself. There must be another reason. And it better be good or his mom and I will ground him 'til spring."

"Ah, cut the kid some slack, Rog," Ranger Karlstad chuckled. "I did the same thing once when I was his age."

"I'll tell you what. You be the one that tells that to my wife. She was sick with worry. Didn't sleep a wink last night. And I didn't do much better."

"I hear you. But no, I'll pass on being the one to tell her."

The men could no longer hear the snowmobile.
"Guess the Springwood kid must have made it," the warden offered. "Listen. I don't hear a thing. Travis must be okay."

* * *

Seth powered up the beach slope bordering the evergreen grove. He killed the engine, pulled off his helmet, and sat in the sudden silence—listening. There was nothing to hear—just the breeze blowing through tree tops.

He cupped his hands to his mouth and shouted. "Travis!"

No reply.

He tried a second time. "Traaaa-vis!"

More silence.

Seth slid off the seat and trudged into the grove. Maybe the smoke was from last night's fire. Maybe his buddy was still sleeping.

The brawny teen stomped into the evergreens, certain he'd find his friend. When he reached the opening, he came to an abrupt halt. The clearing was empty. He stood motionless, surveying the scene. He saw imprints where two tents had dented the snow. And tracks; lots of tracks—footprints from several people.

The fire he was hoping to find was only a pile of smoldering embers. Seth noticed something else. Near where the tents had been pitched were ski tracks. That sort of made sense. The path leading to the lake was a hiking and skiing trail. With weather so mild, it wouldn't be that unusual for a couple of cross-country skiers to stay overnight. Winter camping was becoming a popular activity in the wilderness area.

* * *

The three men marched single file through the snowy boughs. They came to a halt at the edge of the clearing. Roger felt his joy deflate like air from a leaky balloon. Ahead, on the other side of the opening, Seth was bent over, studying something in the snow.

"What d'ya find?" the ranger asked, looking around Roger's wide shoulder.

Seth stood and whirled in one quick motion. He hadn't heard the men approach. "Not Trav," the boy stammered. "But somebody camped here last night. Looks like a couple of cross-country skiers. I was just looking at the tracks. They head out through the woods."

"Really? Ski tracks? Heading into the woods?" Warden Ambroy said, crossing the clearing as he spoke. "By gosh, you're right. Looks like two people stayed over for the night. We must have just missed them. Seems odd, though, that they'd head in that direction. You fellows have any ideas?"

Mr. Larsen's mind was somewhere else. He hadn't heard the question. "What? What did you say?"

The ranger answered. "Ambroy asked if we thought it was odd that the tracks head away from the lake. I don't know. Maybe the skiers think it's shorter to cut through the woods."

"That's possible," the warden agreed. "But they better hope they don't run into a bunch of windfalls back there. They'll be carrying skis, not wearing them."

"What about Travis?" Roger asked. "Do you see any sign that he was here?"

"Kinda hard to tell," the ranger replied. "I suppose it's possible one of those tent dents is his. But he didn't have skis, did he? You said he brought along snow-shoes. I sure don't see any snowshoe tracks."

The warden spoke. "Gentlemen, we need a plan. The weather is supposed to take a turn for the worse. Any suggestions?"

They all went quiet—thinking. It was Seth who came up with the idea. "Maybe I should head back to the trucks and have Rollie get to the nearest phone. I think we should get an air search going right away."

"That makes good sense," the ranger nodded. "Have Rollie call headquarters and tell them we need a full-out Search and Rescue operation. Tell them I'll wait in the truck at the trailhead. I'll monitor the radio on the emergency frequency. Have them call me when a pilot's in the air."

"What about us?" Roger asked. "Shouldn't we keep looking in the meantime?"

"Definitely. You can double up on Ambroy's machine. I'll ride along for a mile or two. If we find your son, he can ride with me. If not, I'll head back to the highway while you two keep looking."

"Sounds like a good game plan," Roger replied, turning to leave. "Let's get moving."

Chapter Nine

CHAPTER NINE

Tired and aching, Travis needed a break before checking the far side of the big pine. He'd already sifted through snow where he'd plopped after the poorly planned flight lesson. Sitting with his back against a support limb, he gazed up. Along the ridge, leafless tree tops were beginning to dance—swaying back and forth to an imaginary rock and roll tempo. He held his breath and listened hard with both ears. The wind had increased enough to rattle branches. He hadn't noticed that earlier. By the way his breath formed puffs of vapor, he knew the temperature had continued to plunge.

He found an opening in the forest canopy where he could study the sky, and realized it too had changed. Earlier, the sky had shown a promise of blue, as if it might eventually turn out to be a sunny day. Low swirling clouds had now taken on the color of dull lead, a gunmetal gray that seemed to be darkening before his eyes.

The last thing needed was more snow. An air search would be useless in a whiteout. Even if planes or copters could fly, snow would reduce visibility, making it difficult to spot smoke. Travis was almost sorry he'd looked up. Now, more than ever, he needed the tool.

Ignoring his hurt, he crawled under the blowdown to continue the hunt.

As fast as he could make them go, his hands swept back and forth, hoping to touch cold steel. Each empty effort brought more concern. When finished with a fruitless scour along the far side of the windfall, he stopped, more uneasy than ever. To help calm the swarm of panic bees buzzing about in his gut, Travis started mumbling to himself. "Okay, okay. You know the tool is here somewhere. It just couldn't fly away. First, go back and feed the fire, check on your company, and come up with a better way to search."

The short hike back to camp wasn't quite so troublesome. A path was being tramped and being so unnerved masked some of the pain. The knee throbbed and ached, but wasn't as paralyzing as it had been earlier. By half limping, half hopping, he made the trip nonstop.

Only a few coals held life. Travis grabbed up a handful of sticks, scattered them on hot ashes, knelt close, and puffed. With help from a few breaths of air, flames soon licked upward and began eating away at the new rations. He breathed easier, and then plopped on the tent fabric, deep in thought. What he needed was a way to sift snow.

His first idea was to remove the twine from the drag. Using a forked branch, he could weave the cord into a web. A second idea took shape: he already had a pair of nets—the snowshoes. The broken frames were useless, but the webbing was still in place. A snowshoe should make a terrific sifting tool. Eager to test his theory, he unhitched the shoes from the carrier, chose the one least damaged, and hobbled his way to the search site.

The prize was hiding directly underneath the giant log. Earlier, and with so much snow, his hands had swept through the area without ever touching metal. When

Travis spotted the tool snagged up in the webbing of the snowshoe, he exhaled a loud sigh of relief. "Gotcha!" he mouthed. He didn't have food, but at least wherever he hiked, he'd have fire.

With the injury, fuel gathering became a grueling task. Part of the problem was not being able to stomp limbs into smaller sections. That had been Travis' usual method of making fire-sized sticks. He would drag a branch close to camp, place one end on a log, and splinter the middle with his feet. But now, with the use of only one good leg, he had to rely strictly on arms and hands. He was pushing a rather tough, unbreakable branch into the flames, when the answer became obvious.

"Wolf, you're hanging out with a blockhead. There's no need to make little pieces. All I gotta do is put one end of a stick in the fire, let the end of the branch hang out like a spoke on a wheel. When enough sticks are stacked on top each other, the pile should burn just fine."

Travis hobbled off to collect more wood. A half-dozen trips later he had enough limbs piled to test his theory. He could picture how it would work. When the butt end of a branch was laid over hot coals, it'd burn like a log in a fireplace—feeding off others. All he should have to do was circle the fire every now and then, pushing unburned portions over hot ashes. There was no need to break limbs into short sections. The fire took care of that chore by itself. Pleased with his idea, Travis stood close, savoring the heat, wondering why he hadn't done it that way before. It sure saved a lot of extra effort.

Following a short rest, Travis went back to gathering wood. But before long the knee begged for relief and he had to quit. Back at camp he slumped on the tent fabric, trying to organize his thoughts, letting the leg relax. It only took minutes for a chill to set in. What he needed was to get out of the wind. The tent would have to be set up.

Later, and after tending the fire, Travis said a few words to the wolf and crawled into the shelter. Just a short nap, he thought. Maybe the leg would be better when he woke up.

* * *

Seth was halfway to the highway when the engine suddenly coughed, sputtered, and quit. That was puzzling—the motor had been ticking away flawlessly. He brushed snow from the fuel gauge and couldn't believe his eyes. The needle had buried itself on empty. How could that be? The tank had been full and he hadn't gone far. Seth flipped up the face shield and was immediately surrounded by the odor of raw gasoline. Not knowing what else to do, he unlatched the hood, and stood staring at the inner workings. Removing a glove, he reached under the motor and dragged his fingers across the belly pan. His hand returned wet and stinky—damp with fuel.

The troubled teenager stared at hoses, wires, and various metal parts. He knew there had to be a leak somewhere between the gas tank and the engine. Scrunching his face closer, he saw problem. A line to one of the two carburetors was dripping. He reached down and felt the fitting. A connection nut was loose— so free he could tighten it with his fingers. "Oh man, what now?" Each word formed a little white cloud as it left his mouth.

Frustrated, he plopped on the snowmobile seat, wondering what to do about it. Only two things made sense. He could wait for the ranger, double-up on the ride to the highway, or he could start off on foot. Walking on top of snowmobile tracks shouldn't be too difficult, even with a weak, untested ankle.

Knowing he'd get overheated walking in full winter gear, he stripped off his parka and bibs, rolled them in a tight ball, and stuck them behind the windshield. With a last look at the useless machine, Seth turned and headed in the direction of the parking area.

It didn't take long to realize that the doctor had been right. He hadn't trudged far before the injured ankle began to ache. That meant he'd have to stop often to rest, but at least he wasn't cold. The unplanned exercise had him breathing hard. He could take short breaks without getting too chilled. Farther up the trail was a windfall—a perfect place to pause. Seth shuffled quietly along until he reached the fallen tree. With an insulated glove, he brushed away snow, settled down, and sat quiet—waiting for the ache to ease.

With rest the ankle began to feel better. Seth was about to stand, when out of the blue, he heard voices. He peered up and down the trail. Empty. More talking— coming from somewhere in the woods. Two men's voices, one high and chirpy, the other deep and raspy, much like a TV wrestler. Seth was about to shout a greeting, then thought better of it. Neither man sounded familiar. Maybe he'd learn something just by listening.

High voice: "Dang-it all, Frank! Slow down! I'm out of wind."

Raspy voice: "Is that all you can do is whine, whine, whine? You cry more than a room full of wet babies. Next time I go huntin', you're staying home."

High voice: "Yeah, good luck. Next time you can tote in your own stinkin' bait. There must have been thirty pounds of sour meat in that pack you made me haul in the other day."

Raspy voice: "You got a hearing problem? Didn't I just say you ain't coming with me next time?"

Seth clearly heard the remark about the meat. These two weren't fishermen or campers. He knew meat was sometimes used to bait animals; possibly bear, coyote, or wolf. But no hunting seasons were open this time of year. These men had to be poachers. Nervous, Seth eased low alongside the trunk of the fallen tree, and then peeked cautiously over the top, hoping to see the men before they saw him. The voices became easier to understand.

High voice: "What's the plan? We gonna cut over to the trail or stay in the woods?"

Raspy voice: "We better stick to the trees—avoid the parkin' lot. People probably waitin' for that kid. We need to stay out of sight, maybe even cross the highway, ski along the other side 'til we get close to the machines."

High voice: "Jeez, that's a lot of extra work. Can't we just say we didn't see him? No one would be the wiser."

Raspy voice: "Hey, so far we've been lucky. Nobody knows we're even here. Why take the chance? It looks like it could snow again. What more can we ask for? Perfect for covering our tracks."

Seth knew he needed to stay concealed. For sure these two would make bad company. And what did they mean about 'the kid'? Had they seen his buddy?

The teen's side vision caught movement. No wonder he hadn't noticed them. They were dressed in white. Even their backpacks were draped with cream-colored towels. With snow covering every tree and bush, they moved through the forest like ghosts. If the men hadn't been talking, they would have slipped by without Seth ever knowing they were near.

Fearful, Seth slouched deeper into the snow, wishing he were invisible. And then he waited, holding his breath, his heart fluttering like a flag in the wind. He gave the men plenty of time to pass, and carefully chanced a look. They were gone. Only thin lines in the snow gave evidence the pair had been real.

Another decision: stay put and wait for the ranger, or continue up trail and hope to reach the highway without being seen? The teen swung his arms up and down, hoping to chase away a sudden chill. Without snowmobile gear, he wasn't dressed warmly enough to sit for very long. The choice was made: best to start hiking. Besides, the men were on skis. He wasn't likely to catch up to them.

* * *

Mrs. Larsen was becoming more distressed by the minute. The early part of the day had been spent sitting by the telephone, hoping for good news. Finally she couldn't stand the suspense. After giving Beth a quick peck on the cheek, she donned her winter jacket, hopped in her car, and headed up the highway.

The drive did nothing to calm her fears. The wind had increased, just like the latest forecast predicted. Through every opening, gust-driven eddies of snow raced across the tarmac, causing the small car to shudder as if pushed by an unseen hand. Linda gripped tight to the steering wheel and said a prayer—not for herself, but for Travis. She prayed her son would be waiting, safe and sound, when she arrived at the trailhead.

Ten minutes later her Honda rolled into the unplowed parking lot. Roger's car sat next to a pair of government pickups, a trail of steam puffing out from the exhaust pipe. The driver's door of the Larsens' wagon swung open and Rollie Kane emerged, a grim look on his face. The elderly resort owner trudged to the Honda, opened the passenger door, and slowly folded himself inside.

The Kris Kringle look-alike managed a small smile, cleared his throat, and tried to put a positive lift to his voice. "Morning, Linda. Didn't expect to see you here."

"Oh, Rollie, I couldn't stand staying home, not knowing what was happening. Any news?"

"Sorry. I haven't seen anyone since they headed out a few of hours ago. I thought by now they'd have sent Seth with a message. Shouldn't take that long to buzz back on a snowmobile."

"What do you think that means? Do you think they found Travis?"

The old man tugged at his beard and studied the view out the side window. "I don't know what to think, Linda. Let's hope it follows that old saying—'no news is good news.'"

"Rollie, look! Somebody's hiking up the trail!" Linda Larsen exclaimed, pointing at the wood-line down the open slope.

"By golly, you're right. From here it looks like Seth. There must be a problem with the snowmobile. And from the way he's limping, it looks like he's been walking a while. Let's go give him a hand."

* * *

Travis awoke cold and worried. How long had he slept? Maybe too long. The fire might be dead. After painfully pulling on boots, Travis clawed his way outside. To his relief, a wisp of smoke remained—a few coals still clinging to life.

With a blaze gnawing away at new fuel, Travis checked the wolf. To the boy's surprise, the yearling was awake and alert. "Man, Midnight. Don't know 'bout you, but my stomach's running on empty. It takes more than a cup of soup to keep my motor going. Guess there's nothing I can do about it. But I'm glad to see one of us is feeling better."

A gust of wind rattled tree tops, diverting the teen's attention. Overhead, naked limbs were shivering before a cold breeze—becoming unwilling swing partners as wrists and arms were pushed and pulled by blasts of arctic air. Real winter weather had arrived.

A second observation—snow was falling. Tiny flakes, small and dry, no bigger than salt crystals. Pangs of anxiety flittered about in Travis' otherwise empty stomach. Making a smoky fire would be futile. Unless a helicopter were to fly directly overhead, it'd be impossible to see the smoke. And wind noise would make yelling useless. Words wouldn't journey farther than the first blowdown.

This was developing into a life-threatening situation. With fire, at least he could warm his body parts. But surviving in frigid weather took lots of extra energy, and he had none to spare. Some way, injured leg and all, he'd have to find something edible. For without food, the poacher's wish would become reality. Come spring, birds would have bones to pick—those of a teenage skeleton.

Returning to the tent, Travis slipped into the bag and propped on an elbow to study the map. He wasn't certain of his location. The hiking trail could be right over the next hill; or it might be miles away. At this point, it didn't really matter. The knee was too tender for travel. There was no way could he tote the pack or pull the drag. And with so much time and effort invested in saving the pup, he wouldn't abandon the animal now.

The map became a blur as eyes watered. Travis hated when that happened. He was far too old to cry. A trickle of tears streaked down his cheeks until he could taste their salty flavor. Taking a deep breath, he struggled to gain control. When the flood had been dammed, he tipped back and stretched the leg, trying to will the ache away. Then, with eyes closed tight, he wracked his brain. What could he find to eat?

Fish? Fish kept him alive on the autumn trip. The chart showed the nearest water to be a creek. Travis remembered crossing the small stream on a crude timber bridge. The creek meandered through a wide valley, connecting several ponds. He had even stopped on the wide, primitive trestle coming in, surprised to see water flowing ice-free.

Maybe, if he could reach the stream, he could catch a brook trout. But trying to catch fish in a shallow creek would be a long shot. Regardless of size, most would have migrated to lakes for the winter. Mulling it over, he didn't see a second choice. He'd spend the rest of this day preparing for tomorrow. If he hadn't been rescued by morning, and if the weather didn't improve, he'd break camp and hobble toward running water.

* * *

Following the close encounter with the poachers, Seth hiked nonstop toward the highway. He was gasping for air, and his ankle was aching, when he caught sight of Rollie and Mrs. Larsen rushing down the hill.

"What in the world happened?" Rollie hollered as they drew near each other. "And where's the Polaris?"

"Quit halfway back. Gas leak," Seth said between gasps.

Mrs. Larsen couldn't wait for a report. Rushing around Rollie, she asked, "Did you find Travis?"

"Nope. Didn't see him. The men are still searching. We need to get to a phone, contact the ranger station. Karlstad wants to call in more help."

Linda let out a small gasp and then grabbed onto Seth's arm. "Wasn't there any sign of him? Didn't you see where he camped?"

"We thought we did. There was a fresh campsite along the lake, but it wasn't made by Trav. The camp was used by two people. We figured it for a couple of cross-country skiers."

Seth was sensible enough not tell Mrs. Larsen everything. He first needed to talk to Rollie—alone. The conversation overheard in the forest was too frightening. "Mrs.

Larsen, Ranger Karlsted wants one of us to phone head-quarters. If it's all right with you, I'd like to stay here and get the snowmobile running. Maybe Rollie can help me."

"Is that okay with you, Linda? You up to driving home and making the call?" the old gentleman asked. "If you're too upset, I can ride along with you."

"No, you stay here. I'll go. But soon as I make the call, I'm coming back. Seth, did the ranger have any special instructions?"

"Yeah. He said they should try to get a plane in the air as soon as possible. He said he'd be returning to the truck to monitor the emergency frequency."

"Anything else I should do before I return?"

"Ah…I hate to ask, but if it's not too much of a hassle, could you bring a can of gas? If you don't have any at your place, there's a can just inside the door of the resort shed."

"I'm sure Roger has a five gallon container in the garage for the snow blower. Anything else?" she asked over her shoulder as she headed for the Honda.

"Thanks. Maybe an apple or an orange and some water. The walk really made me thirsty."

In the parking area, Rollie stood silent, watching Mrs. Larsen pulling out onto the highway. When the car had vanished from sight, he turned to Seth. "So what's really on your mind? Might you know more than you were willing to share with Linda?"

"Rollie, something strange is going on. You won't believe what I'm going to tell you. I think Trav might be in real trouble, but not from the weather."

"Well, boy, try me. I've never known you to not get things right. I trust you more than you realize. If Travis needs our help, we all need to get on it, pronto."

Seth filled Rollie in about the snowmobile and how he had to hike the trail. When he came to the part about skiers weaving through the woods, Rollie interrupted, making sure he was hearing things right. "Let's see if I've got this all straight," Rollie broke in. "There were two guys on skis, staying to the woods, dressed in white, heading for the highway?"

"Yup, but that's not the most important part. I kept hidden so they couldn't see me. The scary part was what they said. They mentioned something about a kid. How they needed to stay out of sight 'til they got to their machines. They had to be talking about Trav. Who else could it have been?"

"You did good," Rollie praised. "Did you happen to get a good look at the men?"

"Not really. I know one was really tall. The other was short and chubby. I could see they both had beards."

"One tall, one short, both with beards. Hmm…doesn't sound like anyone I know. I wonder where they parked their snowmobiles? Maybe we should leave a note on the ranger's windshield. Let him know Linda's calling headquarters. I think you and I better go on a mission of our own."

* * *

The Larsens' SUV rolled slowly along the snow-packed roadway—Rollie at the wheel, Seth in the passenger seat. They were looking for a likely place to temporarily stash a couple of snowmobiles.

Suddenly Seth yelped and pointed to a grove of snow-coated evergreens. "Rollie, stop! Down there, in that clump of young pines! I caught a glimpse of yellow. Maybe those guys drive Skidoos. You know, the old kind with bright yellow hoods."

Rollie pulled the large carryall onto the narrow shoulder and pushed the flasher button. "Are you sure?" He asked, straining to look through the side window.

"Yeah, there's something down there. Want me to take a look?"

"That'd be a good idea. I'll wait here and watch. With all the snow, I think I'd have a hard time hiking up the hill. Think your ankle's up to it?"

"Shouldn't be a problem. It's not that far. I'll be back in a few minutes," Seth said, pushing the door open.

The youth slipped outside and quickly crossed the highway. He trotted up the road and then cut down hill at an angle, heading for the stand of young pines. Rollie put the automobile in reverse and slowly backed along the shoulder. When he was directly opposite the evergreens, he put the gear selector in park and got out. He shuffled across the road just as Seth disappeared into the grove. It made him nervous that he could no longer see his young friend.

The portly senior was about to head down the slope himself when Seth reappeared. Rollie waited patiently as Seth tromped up the hill, knee deep in drifted snow. With a small smile on his face, and clutching something in a gloved hand, the teenager bounded over the plow ridge.

Rollie couldn't wait. "What d'ya find? Was it what you thought?" he shouted before Seth had reached him.

"Yup. A couple of old-style Skidoos. They were covered with a green tarp. Lucky for us the wind caught a corner of the canvas and blew it off one of the machines. Otherwise I'd never have noticed them."

"Guess that means you heard right. These so-called cross-country skiers must be up to no good. Now we've gotta think of a way to stall 'em until we can get a sheriff's squad up here.

"Ah, it shouldn't be too much of a problem keeping those guys around for a while. Hope I don't get in trouble, but I borrowed these," Seth said, opening his fist.

"Why you clever rascal," Rollie laughed. "You're right. Unless they have spares, I don't think they'll get far without sparkplugs."

"Not to worry. I borrowed the spares, too. Both machines had extras tucked in the storage compartment," Seth said, patting the bulge in his pocket. Now I know why you always want me to carry a utility tool on my belt. A person never knows when he'll find a use for it."

"We better get back to the trailhead," Rollie said. "Maybe the men have returned. Both Karlstad and Ambroy have two-way radios in their trucks. They can call in for a sheriff's squad to help sort this thing out."

"Hey, you don't think those guys did something to Trav, do ya?" Seth asked as they were crossing the icy roadway.

"Hard to say. But I think these ski buddies of yours have some questions to answer. And with the way the weather's turning sour, the sooner we get some satisfaction, the better chance Travis will be home in his own bed tonight."

Chapter Ten

C H A P T E R   T E N

The snowmobile search hadn't gone as planned. The three men had unexpectedly run into their own set of problems. After Seth departed, the trio had cruised farther up the hiking trail, hoping to find some evidence Travis had traveled along this route.

The collision occurred while Roger was leaning forward—talking into the warden's ear. "I said, pretty hard to see yesterday's tracks with all this new cover." The warden had twisted his neck to give a reply when they came to a crashing halt—rear-ending the lead machine. Roger and the warden were hurtled off the seat and head first into cold white powder.

"What the…!" Roger blurted, sitting up and brushing icy flakes from his face. Then he saw the cause of the accident. Lumbering into the forest was a large moose. The huge mammal had apparently stepped from behind a windfall and directly onto the trail. The lead driver had no choice but to squeeze the brake. Seeing the big animal, all Roger could add was, "Oh!"

"You guys okay?" Karlstad inquired, extending a hand to both.

"No bones broken. How 'bout you, Rog?" the grizzled warden said, rising on wobbly legs.

"I'm fine," Roger replied. "Can't say the same for the machines. Looks like we have a real doozy of a problem."

The others turned to see what Roger was talking about. The collision had caused the left ski of the rear snowmobile to twist up and over the track of the lead machine. Worse, further inspection revealed that the sprocket of the first machine was damaged beyond repair.

"Dang!" Roger grimaced. "If it's not one thing, it's another. We're not going be of much help to Trav like this. What d'ya think?"

The ranger and warden had dropped to their knees, taking a closer look. Karlstad came up with a suggestion. "Well, I think we'd all agree that my machine's useless. There's no way the track will turn." He hesitated, getting the idea straight in his head. "And the other sled will be impossible to control with only one ski. We'll have to make a switch—put one of my skis on Ambroy's machine."

"Might work," Ambroy agreed. "You got any tools?"

"A few. Some basic ones in the storage nook. A couple of wrenches and a pair of pliers."

"Hey guys, time's a' wasting. We've gotta get a move on. Let's see if we can pull these snow pigs apart," Roger said. "Seems to be getting colder and it looks like it's snowing a bit harder. We need to find Trav before the day gets away from us."

The men went to work. The ski had wedged itself between the track and tunnel and refused to let loose. After a half hour of pushing, pulling, and prying, the men gave up. "It's not going to happen," Roger complained, frustrated at the lack of progress.

"Let's try unbolting it," Ambroy suggested.

"Sure, that'd be simple if we could get at the nut on the other side. The way the ski is jammed in, I don't think we can get a wrench on it," Roger pointed out.

Without proper tools, and with both the bolt and nut badly twisted from the accident, it was another half hour before the men managed what should have been a five minute task. Then more bad luck. Karlstad had unbolted a ski from his machine and was waiting patiently to mount it on the second sled. The problem came when he tried to attach the ski to a different make of snowmobile. The parts didn't match. The flange on the ranger's ski was a little too wide. And no matter how hard they pushed, the ski refused to slip into the other machine's bracket.

"Gentlemen," Roger announced, checking his watch. "We've wasted most the morning trying to make this work. You two can keep struggling. I'm heading back on foot."

"You sure you want to do that?" Ambroy asked, looking up. "The trucks are miles from here. That's quite a hike."

"Well, if you get the snowmobile fixed, you can come by and pick me up. For that matter, you two can both ride back to the parking area. You can send Seth in for me on the Polaris."

Ranger Karlstad stood and looked thoughtfully down the trail. "Speaking of Seth," he began, and then stopped to do some mental calculations. "It should have only taken him a few minutes to reach the highway. I'd kinda thought he'd be coming back right away. You don't suppose he found Travis, do you?"

"Maybe, hope you're right," Ambroy answered, pulling on gloves. "Been so busy with the snowmobiles, I forgot about the Springwood kid. Now that I think of it, that machine he's riding is big and powerful. It's probably gutsy enough to pull these clunkers out of the woods. The sixty-four dollar question would be—so where'd he go?"

"That's an important thought, but I don't have the answer," Roger replied. "You two can keep working on the snowmobiles. I'm out of here."

* * *

Roger was becoming soaked inside from perspiration and outside as snow melted on his clothing. Even with long legs, and the partially packed tracks of the snow-mobiles, walking was hard work. His jacket was unzipped—the collar of his shirt unbuttoned.

The rangy wildlife expert trekked forward with swift, high-sweeping steps, lost in a fog of thought. He couldn't help but think Travis may have fallen through the ice—that the search on land was useless. And if Travis had drowned, how would they ever know for sure? They wouldn't be able to drag the lake until after ice out.

The thought of searching the cold waters of the lake made him wince. He had been so quick to say 'yes' to the overnight outing. What was he thinking? If Travis had fallen through the ice, Roger had no one to blame but himself. After the close call in October, he should have just said 'no.' His son would have had many days in the future to go exploring. Maybe now he had none, Roger concluded—his head a whirlpool of emotions—his body pacing down the narrow trail on cruise-control.

* * *

Linda Larsen's Honda rolled into the parking area only moments after Rollie and Seth had done the same in the Chevy wagon. Rollie turned to Seth. "Let's keep mum on this latest development. I'll make an excuse to drive to the resort for a tool or two. I'll call the sheriff's office from there."

"What should I tell her?" Seth asked, leaning forward in his seat for a better look at the Honda.

"Just say you're waiting for one of the other snowmobiles to return. Tell her it's too far up the trail to hike to the Polaris on foot. Now go ahead, get in her car before she gets out and comes over here."

Seth did as he was told. Sliding into the smaller automobile, he pasted a smile on his face and said, "Did you happen remember to grab an apple or an orange?"

"Yes, I did. There's one of each in the bag," Mrs. Larsen answered, pointing to a brown paper sack on the seat beside her. Looking out the passenger window, she asked, "Where's Rollie going with the wagon?"

"Ah...we forgot to tell you we needed a special tool to fix the gas line. Rollie's running to the resort to get it. He thought I should wait here with you 'til he gets back."

Linda turned to read the young man's face. "There's something you're not telling me, isn't there? Seth, I've known you since you were a baby. I can tell when you're hiding something. What is it? What do you know that I don't?"

Seth turned his head and pretended to watch the big boxy vehicle disappear down the highway. "Nothing, really," he mumbled. "We're not sure what's going on. Rollie just said to wait here with you. He thinks the others should be back any minute."

"Seth, I sense there's more than you're telling me. If you know something I don't, I want to hear it now. All of it."

"Honest, Mrs. Larsen. I don't know what's going on. I just know Trav can take care of himself."

"I wish I felt as confident as you," she answered, a tear trickling from the corner of one eye. "Why do you boys have to take these dangerous adventures? Why can't you be content to sit at home and watch TV at night like other kids your age?"

Her comment surprised Seth. "Do you really mean that? Would you rather Trav stay home and be a couch potato?"

"Oh, never mind. I'm upset and more than a little worried. No, I don't want you guys to become couch potatoes. But couldn't you two pick better weather to be out playing in?" Linda asked, trying to force a smile.

"I guess you'll have to ask Mother Nature about that," Seth answered, staring out the window. "It seems she likes to pull surprises on us."

For the next half hour the two sat quietly, each in their own world. They were gazing out the snow-dappled windshield and failed to realize Rollie had returned. He pulled alongside the Honda, powered down the window, and yelled in a booming voice. "Why don't you two come sit in here? There's more room. I'll put it in four-wheel drive and pull to top of the hill to get a better view."

When they were seated in the big wagon—Linda Larsen in the front, Seth in the rear—Rollie decided it was time to share. From old habit, he stroked his neatly trimmed whiskers and cleared his throat. "Linda, I didn't get to hear what you learned from the call to the ranger station. Can we expect to have company soon?"

"Not right away," she answered. "Because of the holidays, most of the staff is out of town. The only pilot on emergency call lives in Ely. What is that by air, fifty, sixty miles, maybe more?

"Something like that," Rollie agreed.

"Anyway, the woman I talked to said it's snowing even harder there. She wasn't sure the pilot would go up today. She said it was probably too risky, and besides, with the snow, he wouldn't see much."

"Kinda what I figured. But in a few minutes a couple of deputies should arrive. After that, some of the Search and Rescue people should be here with snowmobiles, skis, and snowshoes."

"Oh, thank God!" Linda exclaimed. "It's about time. Wait. How do you know all that? You went back to the resort for more than a tool, didn't you?"

"Yup, I did," Rollie admitted. "Talked to the boss sheriff, himself. Lucky for us that Seth had trouble with the snowmobile. While hiking back to the trucks, he learned something we need to share with you."

"Oh dear! What is it? Is it news about Trav? Why didn't you tell me before?" Linda interrupted in a voice wrought-up with emotion.

"Calm down, Linda. The answer is yes and no. It's about Travis. But it's not necessarily bad news."

Rollie told of what Seth had heard, softening the words the skiers had used. When he was through, Mrs. Larsen sat open-mouthed, not knowing what to think. After a long pause, she suddenly blurted, "We have to find those men! If they have information about Trav's whereabouts, we need to know right now!"

"That's why the deputies will be here soon," Rollie replied, his voice calm and level. "Thanks to some creative thinking by Seth, those two fellows shouldn't get far. Seth spotted their snowmobiles hidden in some pines down the road a ways."

Rollie turned to face the rear. "Seth thought that maybe changing sparkplugs in the Polaris would help get it started."

"What? I don't get it," Mrs. Larsen said, a puzzled look on her face.

"Show Linda what you borrowed, boy. I think she'll get a better picture of what we're talking about."

Seth dug into his pocket and pulled out a sparkplug. He held it up for Mrs. Larsen to see. For the first time since entering the car, a hint of a grin played on her lips. "Oh, now I understand. Unless those two plan on skiing home or wherever they're headed, they'll need new plugs to start their engines."

"Right," Rollie chuckled softly. "Once we explain that to the deputies, all they have to do his hide out near the snowmobiles and wait. We can let the law find out just what those two have to share."

"Speaking of the law," Seth announced. "A couple of squads are pulling in right now."

With keen interest, the deputies listened as Seth retold the story. He related everything but the part where he had removed the sparkplugs. Once the officers had gathered the information, they left to make a plan in the privacy of a patrol car. Several minutes later they returned to the Suburban.

The older of the two, a thin, wiry man in his fifties, spoke first. "From what you've told us, we really don't have enough reason to make an arrest. We'll park down the road and wait. We can question them, but that's about all we can do. Chances are they'll have an alibi— truthful or not."

"Yep," continued the second officer, a stocky, dark-haired woman in her late thirties or early forties. "Too bad there's not some way we could keep them in the area for a while. Unless we find some type of violation, after we ask a few questions, they'll be free to leave."

Rollie winked at Seth. "Ah, yes. Those two so-called skiers might be here a little longer than they figured. My young friend here tells me that when he checked their snowmobiles, both were missing sparkplugs."

"Well, that's interesting," the older officer said, a sly grin creasing the corners of his weathered cheeks. "Maybe someone did us a favor."

The woman deputy glanced at her watch. "Best we get moving. On skis, those two fellows may have already made it to their machines. Besides, with the search team on their way, it's going to get crowded up here. Most of the rescue volunteers will be driving pickups. There'll be a parade of trucks and trailers parked along the edge of the road."

She turned and spoke directly to Mrs. Larsen. "You must be worried sick. We'll let you know whatever we learn. Let's all keep our fingers crossed. Maybe Travis will walk out on his own. From what I remember from last fall, he knows how to handle himself in the woods."

Linda nodded once and held up her hands. "I've had my fingers crossed since the moment Travis left home. Doesn't seem to help, though, does it? He's still missing."

* * *

Knowing full well there might be vehicles in the parking area, the poachers stayed to the woods. When they were within a few hundred yards of the highway, they crossed over the trail and skied silently on. Once away from the path, they stopped to take a breather.

"Can't be too many people out looking for that kid," the tall poacher grunted to his panting partner. "Those snowmobile tracks we crossed are hours old. Woulda thought there'd be a whole mess of people runnin' up and down the trail by now."

"Don't be gettin' too cocky," wheezed his chunky cohort. "Maybe the kid lied to us. Maybe he wasn't supposed to be home for another day or two."

"Ya know, Rusty, I think maybe you're on to something. Sure, he had snowshoes and a fishing rig. He probably wasn't expected back until sometime today. Hey, that's good news for us. We're home free and clear."

"Maybe. But Frank, when we get close to the machines, let's hide the wolf pelt. If no one's around, you can run back and get it. Better safe than sorry."

"You been smoking something new in that old pipe of yours? You've said two things in a row that make perfect sense. Of course I'm gonna ditch the hide. The rifle, too."

"Frank, I'm gonna try goin' three for three. If we do get questioned, how 'bout we say we met the kid a couple days ago. Say he was planning on walking the south shore of the lake all the way to the end. Say he told us he was gonna camp there and take another trail out."

"Hey! What's with you? That's a great idea. Trail 128 comes out miles down the road. When the searchin' becomes hot and heavy, they'll be lookin' in the wrong place. They'll never find that smart mouth punk, 'specially with all this snow."

The two scofflaws began skiing again. It wasn't until they had to halt to climb over a windfall did the plump poacher make his fourth observation. "But Frank, I gotta tell ya, this whole thing bothers me. Bothers me a bunch. We came out here for a wolf skin, not to kill some kid."

The lanky outlaw threw down his poles and whirled, a loathsome look on his face. With a sudden lunge, he reached out and wrapped both hands around the stout man's throat. "Now hear me and hear me good! I ain't

113

about to go back to jail for killing one lousy wolf. So forget about that kid. If he dies, it's his own damn fault. Boy like that should know better than be hiking the woods in the middle of the winter."

The shorter man struggled to free himself. He threw his arms up, trying to break his partner's grip. Just then, the long-legged poacher released his hold, and with a quick thrust, pushed his struggling accomplice backwards. The stubby man plopped seat first in the snow. Shocked and red-faced, he sat gasping for air, staring up, as if seeing his friend for the very first time.

Without another word, the tall man spun around, picked up his skiing gear, and continued climbing over the fallen tree. Shaking his head in disgust, the plump fellow pushed up, brushed himself off, and followed behind.

Soon they could see the evergreen plantation where they'd stashed the snowmobiles. The lean poacher stopped to remove the backpack. After releasing the rolled up tent and sleeping sack, he opened the top storage compartment and pulled out the wolf pelt.

The man took a moment to locate a hiding spot they would easily remember. Nearby a tree had toppled— bundled roots and all. "Over there," he directed, pointing at the overturned aspen. "Let's cover the rifle and fur at the base of that tree. The Skidoos can't be more than a hundred yards from here."

The men stuffed the pack containing the wolf skin and rifle parts into a plastic sack. With his boot, the long-legged outlaw cleared snow from the hollow of the upturned root. He knelt, set the bag into the hole, and then pushed powder over the shiny surface.

Wearing an evil grin of satisfaction, the man stood tall before barking out the next order. "We need to get to the snowmobiles and get the gear tied down. When we're sure the coast is clear, I'll swing back and retrieve our package. With any luck, we'll be home free."

* * *

Roger Larsen scowled as he looked at his watch. It was almost the middle of the afternoon—only a couple of hours of daylight remained. The hike to the highway was taking far longer than he'd first imagined. He gritted his jaw and hurried his pace.

As Roger stomped around a sloping curve, he spotted the outline of Seth's snowmobile. A thin quilt of white blanketed the seat and hood. Roger knew immediately this was not good news. It meant Seth was delayed in relaying the message to send help. Upset and anxious, the usually composed man spat out a curse. What should have been a simple search was fast unraveling into a disaster. He glanced up at the sky. The clouds overhead seemed angrier—more threatening. All he could do was hope Travis had already arrived to the safety of the automobile.

Reaching the disabled machine, and needing a brief rest, Roger cleared the seat with a gloved hand and perched on the padded cushion. He'd just sat down when the distant whine of a snowmobile engine broke the silence. He waited a beat or two, listening, then stood up and leaned against a large tree. Moments later the warden and ranger, doubled up on one sled, came motoring around the curve.

Seeing the abandoned snowmobile, the driver pulled to the side of the trail. Only then did he see Mr. Larsen leaning against a giant aspen. With a extra burst of power, the operator steered the sled around the Polaris, stopped, and killed the engine.

Warden Ambroy gave Roger a shake of his head. "I guess we weren't the only ones to have mechanical problems."

"That's the way it looks," Roger replied. "At least you were able to fix the ski. What took you so long?"

"Actually it didn't take all that much time to make the ski fix. I used a rock as a hammer and bent the bracket a bit wider. Would you believe we had another dilemma? When Earl went to start the engine, the recoil rope broke. We had to take the whole assembly apart and retie the cord," Karlstad explained.

"Yeah. We'd have been here a lot sooner if we had better tools. The wrench was the wrong size. Had to do the whole repair with a pair of pliers," Ambroy added.

Karlstad turned and stared at the snow-draped snowmobile. "Wonder what's wrong with the kid's machine? Did you get a chance to scope it out?"

"No," Roger answered. "Just got here. There's a gassy smell near the hood, must be a fuel leak. But we don't have time to mess with it. One of us needs to get back to your truck and use the radio."

"Can't be that far from here," Ambroy observed. "The Springwood boy must have called for help by now. I'll drop Karl off at the parking area and come right back for you."

With a swift pull of the starter rope, the engine coughed to life. Roger stood off to one side, watching, as the heavily loaded machine wallowed through the thick carpet and disappeared around the next bend. Exhaling a deep breath, he high-stepped onto the snowmobile track, and resumed trekking toward the trailhead.

Chapter Eleven

Travis spent the rest of that murky, snow-filled day preparing for a long winter evening. He was fortunate to have camped in an area filled with windfalls. And although he didn't have to go far for fuel, gathering fire material was a slow and painful process. Every second step was agony, and he had to stop often to rest. Much of what he collected was fed directly to his warm friend—the hungry fire. It had taken several hours of hard work before enough wood was stacked to keep a blaze burning throughout the night.

Several times the wolf had attempted to stand—only to learn that its hind legs weren't ready for travel. Travis felt sorry for the animal. Twice he'd used one of his large mittens to give the yearling water. And whenever the teen was close to camp, he kept up a continual one-sided dialogue. For some unknown reason he felt more hopeful when he chattered aloud. He didn't feel quite so all alone.

That entire afternoon, as the teenager labored on an empty stomach, the wind rattled and whistled in tree tops. It seemed to Travis, as the temperature dropped, the gusts became bolder, and the snow had thickened. Earlier, when he was collecting firewood, the flakes had been small and grainy, hardly a bother. Now, as Travis crouched by the flames, he realized that the flakes had grown. They were collecting again, enough so the little green tent had taken on a milky-colored coating.

"What d'ya think, Midnight? Is Ma Nature going to treat us to a batch of real winter weather?" Travis spoke the words with fake confidence. His fear, like the ground cover, was growing ever deeper. There hadn't been blizzard-like conditions yet this winter. The region was way overdue for some bad weather. In this part of Minnesota, snow events, along with bitter temperatures, could last for days, sometimes longer. Despite the heat from the fire, the thought of a fierce storm gave Travis the chills.

The wintry carpet continued growing thick—flake by flake. If the snow kept up at this rate, Travis feared, it would soon be too deep for hiking. Fidgety, and needing something to keep his mind occupied, he crawled into the tent, unhitched the snowshoes from the pack-frame, and returned to the fire.

There he carefully inspected the broken frames. The snowshoes might well be the only way out. He wrenched his brain—seeking a way to make a fix. For certain he'd have to cut the drag apart. Every scrap of twine and cord would be used. But first, he'd need a couple of curved branches. The limbs would have to be thick enough not to break—yet thin enough to bend.

Maple branches would flex and yet be tough enough not to splinter. Travis scanned the hillside, hoping to find a maple that could be robbed of a limb or two. No luck. Maple trees weren't that common in the BWCAW. Most of the surrounding forest was made up of birch and aspen, with the occasional pine or spruce scattered here and there.

Not far from camp a slender birch had tipped with its roots still attached. A branch from this tree might still be green, and when heated, Travis figured, be fairly flexible. Using the survival tool's saw blade, he cut four small limbs, each about the thickness of his thumb.

Hobbling close to the fire, Travis explained the plan to his campmate. "Here's what I'm gonna do, Midnight. I'll heat up these limbs. While they warm themselves, we'll take apart your sled. I need the rope to fix the snow-shoes. If I get the shoes fixed, maybe I can figure out a way to pull you on that slab of pine. Otherwise, I'm afraid one of us might have to stay behind."

He was able to salvage all the twine and cord. Once certain the branches had thawed, he toted everything to the tent. His idea was to lash the birch limbs to the top of the frames, bridging the cracked and splintered sections. It seemed like a good idea and he worked dili-gently at it most of the afternoon.

There were several unforeseen problems. The first glitch was that the birch limbs had stayed stiff and uncooper-ative. They refused to follow the curved ends of the frames. The second difficulty was that no matter how hard he tugged, Travis wasn't able to pull the twine tight enough to keep the limbs from wiggling. Another issue arose. There wasn't enough of the nylon cord.

Travis didn't trust the twine to take the abuse the frames would get tromping in snow. Unless the new limbs were tied snug and secure, they'd work their way free, making the shoes useless. After many attempts, the youth became totally frustrated. He threw the shoe in a corner of the tent and crawled outside.

Snow had continued falling—even faster then before. During the time he had been working inside, another inch had been added to the landscape. Except now, despite being blocked by trees and blowdowns, the flurries were dropping at an angle. The wind had found a way to reach the forest floor.

119

This was beginning to look more and more like the real thing—a genuine Minnesota blizzard. A nasty snowstorm that even an experienced winter camper would want to avoid. A storm that could easily end the life of a hungry, injured youth—lost and frightened—far from home.

How had he gotten himself into this dilemma, he pondered, trying to push down the panic that was clawing to get out. All he had wanted to do when he'd left home was a little fishing and spend a pleasant night in the woods—proving to himself he could handle it.

If it hadn't been for the wolf killers, he thought, I would be home, safe, secure, full of food, looking at the snow through warm window glass. Then his mind raced ahead to horrible conclusions. Because out here alone, I'm truly terrified. This might be where I die. If I don't get out soon, I'm going to be dead right here and no one will ever find me. I'm going to be crow food, just like that creepy poacher predicted.

The cold, hungry camper knelt by the coals—staring at everything—seeing nothing—his mind a mixture of chaotic thoughts. The ache in his leg was forgotten as he sobbed quietly, knowing that without food, and a way to hike through the ever-deepening ground cover, he was doomed.

The wolf made a small whine, bringing Travis out of his musings. The boy stared at the animal. Could he do it? Could he possibly bring himself to kill such a magnificent creature? Slice through the lush black fur to get at the meat? He wasn't certain; maybe in the morning. Maybe when he could no longer bear the hunger pains, he could make the decision then. But not tonight. Tonight they would share the coming darkness as campmates.

Travis was just about to push himself up for one last firewood gathering, when Mother Nature gave him an unexpected gift. The youth was staring out, wondering which way to head for fuel, when he was startled by movement.

First one, then another, and finally a third brown blur plummeted to earth from a roost high in a tall aspen. Dropping like rocks, three grouse plunged head first into the soft, fluffy quilt, and like magic, vanished. The young outdoorsman had read how these game birds buried themselves in snow for the night, but he'd never actually seen them do it.

Hope surged. If he could locate the holes, maybe he could kill one of the birds. Travis bent to pick up a fire limb, never taking his eyes from where the grouse had disappeared. Then, like a predator stalking prey, he hobbled, quiet step by quiet step, to their entry area.

Three small dents marred the otherwise smooth surface. Travis lifted the limb high and swung down with all his might. He hopped forward, and just as a grouse tried to take flight, whipped the crude club a second time. The limb struck the bird with the force of a shotgun blast, scattering feathers into the air as if a pillow had been slashed. There was no time for a third swat. Almost as if it were fired from a cannon, the last bird shot skyward and was quickly out of range.

Travis pushed the stick into the snow until it touched something soft and rubbery. He brushed away the frosty covering and broke into a wide grin. He had made a direct hit. Looking like it might be napping, the fat brown bird lay in its bed, its head twisted to one side. Success. He had batted two for two.

Mouth watering, Travis looked on in hungry anticipation as meat sizzled over the fire. Having never roasted a chicken before, he was unsure how to prepare the plump little game hens. First he'd spent time plucking feathers. When only a few remained, he used the knife to slit the birds' stomachs and remove the insides. He let the intestines plop into his cooking pot, threw in the small lifeless heads, and set the pan aside. His thinking was, that if the yearling was half starved, it wouldn't be finicky about gulping down the unappetizing innards.

After whittling sharp points on two branches, Travis pushed the sticks through the middle of each bird. With the help of other limbs, he propped the bodies close to the fire. Then he watched, fascinated, as flames licked and burned the few remaining feathers. Once the skin began to char, he moved the birds away from the direct heat. He wanted to make certain the bodies were cooked inside as well as out.

Satisfied the meat was secure and simmering slowly, Travis turned to the pup. "Well, little wolf. Hope you like grouse guts. It's all you're gonna get today."

With a gloved hand, Travis scooped out a fistful of messy insides from the pot. He knelt on his good knee, slowly brought the unappetizing mix to the wolf's muzzle. The animal studied the offering for a short moment, looked up at Travis with large eyes, and then quickly snatched the glob off the mitten. With one quick gulp, the mouthful of bird parts disappeared.

The wolf never hesitated on the second helping. The small handful of intestines vanished faster than the first. Even the feathered heads were wolfed down. "Midnight, where are your manners? You didn't even say thank you," Travis said with the second smile of the day. "Now that you've had something to eat, don't be looking for more. Those two little hens cookin' over there are all mine."

The flesh was light and rather dry, but Travis didn't take notice. A juicy steak couldn't have tasted better. As he sat picking the last of the meat from the delicate bones, he took stock of what he had eaten the past three days.

Since having an early breakfast Monday morning, he came up with a total of four bars, the lake trout fish fillets, and now the meat from two grouse. No wonder I'm hungry, he mused, moving closer to the fire. I ate that much on Christmas Day alone.

Warm, and almost content, Travis didn't sit long. He remembered that the water bottle needed filling. Struggling to his feet, he picked up the pan, cleaned it with snow, packed more white stuff inside, and hung the pan over the flames. Finished, he stared out at his surroundings.

The afternoon light was dull and gray, and with the gloom caused by falling snow, he couldn't see far. A sudden blast of frigid air bullied its way through the protection of the tree top wind break. The tent fabric shuddered violently and a corner of the small shelter lifted as if threatening to leave on its own accord. For a brief moment Travis thought the tent might become a tree house. Fortunately the backpack inside provided enough heft to bring the shelter back to earth.

"Shoot!" Travis spat into the steadily increasing gusts. "Better find a way to hold that thing down before it heads home without me." After tugging several birch tops to the tent, and using as little twine as possible, he tied the corners to the thick end of the limbs.

With the tent secure, the weary teen trudged off for more fuel. The fire had a hearty appetite. Feeding it took lots of time and energy. Finished with the last load, Travis looked up to discover dusk had fallen over the forest.

Enduring the long, dark hours to come would be a cold challenge. The first evening had been balmy. The second night had been frightening, but with high hopes of being rescued, and so tired from the day's travel, he'd slept undisturbed for hours. This night would be different. He couldn't expect to find visitors outside in the morning, waiting to take him home. For certain he was on his own, at least until the weather improved.

"But I'm not starving," Travis reflected, aware the wolf was staring at him from its bed under the blowdown. "What d'ya think, Midnight? You gonna spend the night tucked under that tree, or would you rather sleep in the tent?"

For an answer, the yearling cocked its ears, tipped its head, and stared at the boy.

"You think we're good enough friends to become room-mates?" Travis continued, limping around the fire. "Let's see how it goes. Just don't tell me you snore."

Getting the animal into the shelter was far easier than expected. With the wolf curled on the vest, Travis was able to grasp the padded collar and pull the garment like a sled. Twice the pup tried to stand, but Travis paused, talking all the while, until the animal calmed. When they reached the tent, the youth crawled in, turned around, and pulled the vest inside, wolf and all. He slid his new roommate to one side of the entry, brushed the animal's back several times, then went out to tend the fire.

As dusk turned the corner to dark, the teen stood in the fire's glow, wondering what else he should do. Nothing. There was not a thing he could do but wait for morn-ing, and hope for the best. Taking a last look at the blaze, he dropped to all fours and crawled into the tent.

Chapter Twelve

C H A P T E R   T W E L V E

Daylight hours in the dead of winter are a little like a roller coaster ride. The sun just seems to start its climb, and in a blink or two, it's all over. That notion was one of many Travis conjured as he cuddled in his bag, trying to sort out his situation.

A sudden gurgling noise startled the teen, and for a brief moment, quickened his pulse. Yet, despite all his worries, he couldn't keep from smiling. He wasn't alone. He did have company.

Travis curled up his legs, wondering why his feet felt so frigid. Except for the first day on the ice, cold feet hadn't been an issue. He knew the tent was good for blocking the wind and keeping out snow. But it offered no defense against freezing temperatures. He stayed in a tucked position, rubbing his toes together, deliberating how to keep a bit of body heat inside the little shelter. Certainly fire wasn't the answer. The tent fabric would ignite—not to mention the smoke.

The new snow was much too soft for igloo making. That idea was quickly tossed aside. Travis recalled the times Seth and he had made snow forts. They'd tunnel into the miniature mountain the snowplow had pushed up at the end of the driveway. Inside always seemed much warmer than outside, especially if there was a wind. Rolling that thought around in his head sparked an idea.

Slipping out of the bag, Travis painfully struggled into parka and boots. He hobbled to the fire, added a few sticks, and waited for flames to flare. From up on the ridge came the sound of wind moaning in tree tops— swirling into every crack and corner of the forest. Icy flakes nipped at his cheeks, some stinging like paper cuts, urging Travis to pull down the face mask before rummaging about in the snow.

"Yes," he announced out loud, touching one edge of the board with a gloved hand. The pine slab was about the right size. It could be used both as a plow or crude shovel.

With help from the plank, Travis pushed and pulled snow to all sides of the tent. After three or four scoops, he'd use the flat side of the board to pack snow in place. He worked for the better part of an hour—the blaze providing a flickering night light. Work didn't stop until the shelter was almost completely covered. Only the dome and the door remained exposed.

Back inside the tent, snuggled in the bag, Travis couldn't believe the difference. Besides less wind noise, the interior felt warmer—almost cozy compared to the frigid wind chill factor out in the open. But the thick coating created a change he hadn't considered. The snowy layer blocked light. He wouldn't know when the flames died. Even now, with the fire still burning bright, the inside of the tent was an inky black. Travis fumbled with a parka pocket, pulled out the flashlight, and flicked its beam on his tent partner. The pup was asleep—its tail curled over its nose. Wishing he could do the same, Travis scrunched up as much as the leg would allow, closed his eyes, and tried to think only pleasant thoughts.

As he had often imagined while stranded by the autumn storm, he pictured sitting at the kitchen table—a steaming stack of French toast in front of him, waiting to be smothered under gobs of warm maple syrup. He imagined watching a movie on TV—a big bowl of buttered popcorn warming his lap. And he thought about family and friends—especially Katie. What was she doing right now? Probably on the phone—chatting up a storm—sharing secrets with a girlfriend.

Girlfriend—now there's a word with a couple of meanings, he mused. Was Katie his girlfriend? He thought so, but wasn't sure. They hadn't done much together except sit side-by-side at a couple of high school football games. That, and tease each other most afternoons on the bus ride home. So why did he always feel so strange when he was around her? And how come he became so tongue-tied that often his words tumbled out garbled and mish-mashed? Probably 'cause I'm a moron, he thought. Probably the same reason I'm stuck out here: I make stupid choices. Think of something else. Think of falling asleep.

But sleep wouldn't come easy. The longer he laid thinking, the harder it was to fight off fear. At least in October he had been camped at the edge of a lake. Small fish were plentiful and easy to catch. For over a week, small bass and perch kept him nourished. This dilemma was different—much different. This time there was no lake outside the tent. And most animals were curled up in dens, riding out the winter. Killing the two grouse had been dumb luck. A person could camp an entire lifetime without ever having a chance like that again.

He recalled how Seth and he had survived the first night following the storm. Seth had a broken ankle, the forest around camp was a tangle of windfalls, and a bear had raided the food supply. Yet somehow he'd found courage to comfort Seth. "Let's just take one night at a time," he had preached to his injured partner. "We'll deal with tomorrow when it comes."

"Only thing I can do," Travis whispered to the cold, dark ceiling. "All I can do is to take one night at a time." He forced himself to have warm, pleasant thoughts until exhaustion took over and nudged him into slumber.

He woke several hours later—shivering—unsure of where he was. For a moment he tried to stay still, holding his breath, clearing his head. The snowy mattress below the thin tent floor quickly reminded him of his predicament. The inside of the shelter was an unlighted cave—pitch black. So dark, Travis couldn't tell if his eyes were open or closed. He felt for the flashlight, clutched it, and then rolled on his side, willing his leg to respond.

With effort, he moved the hand grasping the little lantern, and focused the beam on the wolf. The animal was curled in a tight ball—sleeping, obviously equipped for the elements. Travis switched off the light and the tent seemed even darker than before. He lay chilled, wondering if he should venture outdoors and check to see if the fire could be kindled.

Cold, stiff, and mostly by feel, he struggled into the bibs and parka. He'd slithered into the sleeping bag without wearing them. He had read somewhere that in frigid temperatures it was foolish to sleep wearing full winter gear. As a person slumbered, inner clothing would become moist from body vapor. And in below zero weather, wet fabric could be deadly. Yeah, that may be true, Travis reasoned, but I think I'd feel a whole lot warmer wearing everything I own. And for certain, crawling out of the bag would be so much more comfortable.

The blanket of white crystals reflected enough light to illuminate silhouetted shapes of trees. Like tiny missiles, wind-driven flakes stung his cheeks and chin, and he paused to pull down the mask before checking the fire. A close call—only a few feeble embers remained.

On two arms and one knee, Travis pawed until a mitten-covered hand located an unburned branch. One limb at a time, he placed charred sections over the hot coals. Satisfied the fire would flare up, he scooted inside the tent. Back in the bag he couldn't stop from shivering. In just the few minutes he had been out, frigid air had penetrated the sleeping sack. Besides being cold, his knee throbbed, adding to his discomfort. He was truly miserable.

Later that night, and though he knew he might regret the decision, Travis gave up on tending the fire. It was just too much work—caused too much pain. Because once he left the warmth of the bag, he became numb with cold, and couldn't keep from shaking. Come first light, all he could hope for was to find a hot coal or two so he wouldn't have to start over from scratch.

The terrified young camper spent that frigid, unending night dozing, waking, worrying, but mostly shivering. Like being stuck in traffic, time slowed to a crawl and stopped. Finally, after what seemed an eternity, dull light started seeping through the dome, bringing with it mixed relief.

Though daylight was near, the wind hadn't eased. If anything, it was blowing harder than the previous evening. Travis could hear angry gusts shaking and scolding tree limbs up on the ridge. This was not the weather he prayed would greet him come sunrise. Chilled to the bone, he stayed tucked deep in the bag, waiting for more light to leak inside. Rolling over a few minutes later, he was surprised to see the wolf awake, amber eyes unblinking—staring at him.

"Morning wolf. Say, how do you guys do it? Sleep out all year long? That coat of yours must be mighty warm," Travis stammered through chattering teeth. "No answer, huh? So be it. I better get up and at 'em," he continued, working the bag's zipper.

But getting 'up and at 'em' was easier said than done. Overnight the knee had stiffened. Pulling on bibs and boots proved to be a very painful exercise. Twice the teenager had to stop, grit his teeth, and wait for the hurt to pass.

Once fully dressed, he crawled to the door, only to find a new dilemma. During the night, snow had drifted over the tent. Travis had to scoop and push with gloved hands to keep cold powder from spilling inside. Once the door was cleared, he slid out on his belly, anxious to relieve himself. Standing upright was another lesson in pain management. The previous day, though agonizing, the leg had been useable. But in the gray light of early morning, the knee, swollen and unbending, wouldn't follow directions.

He hopped a few steps on one leg. Then, after completing nature's call, took a look at his surroundings. In every direction the landscape was a milky smudge. The snow event had continued all night long. Except for the warm center, almost a half foot of white blanketed the fire circle.

He fought to keep down the rising panic. In such wintry conditions, there was little chance he could be spotted from the air. Best to get the fire going, melt some snow, work on the snowshoes, hope being upright would limber the leg. Turning to face the tent, Travis was surprised and pleased. The pup was standing in the door opening. On three legs, the yearling hobbled forward in the boy's boot tracks, stopped, and peed.

"Well, it's about time you got up," Travis said, his voice sounding frail, even to himself. "You've been lazy long enough."

Removing a glove, Travis scratched the wild dog behind the ears. "Wolf, we have a problem. Those two birds weren't nearly enough to fill the hole in my middle. If you weren't so crippled, I'd send you out to catch a rabbit. I believe it's your turn to find a meal."

The pup stood without moving until Travis stopped scratching, then stood tall on three legs to put its nose in the air.

"What? You smell something?" Travis asked, turning his face to the wind. "Whatever it is, we better hope it comes to us. 'Cause we sure ain't gonna go chasing after it."

After taking a second sniff, the yearling whined, turned, and limped to the tent. "Sure, go back to bed," the boy chided, knowing one problem had solved itself. Because now, if he decided to head for the highway, the wolf could follow on its own. Traveling that direction might be the only chance of reaching help. But first there were things to do. He needed to restart the fire, fill the water bottle, and work at getting the leg to bend.

Every simple chore took longer than expected. Travis was scarcely able to move with enough speed and energy to stay warm. He did have a bit of good luck. Surviving deep under the fire ashes were several hot coals. With the help of dead pine needles and shavings, the embers were brought back to full life.

Once the snow pot hung over the fire, he started breaking camp. Packing up the tent posed a real problem. It was completely buried under its igloo shaped covering. After removing the packframe, and coaxing the yearling outside, the teenager made an extraordinary observation. The snow packed with the board remained firm and rigid. So solid, he was able to fold the tent without worry the igloo shell would collapse.

Travis recalled a fun field trip. One February, several years earlier, the sixth grade class had spent a week at an outdoor education camp. Besides being taught how to walk on snowshoes, the students had made snow huts. The instructor had demonstrated how to make a huge snow mound using snowshoes as shovels.

A few hours later, they'd returned to find the mound stiff and as solid as if it had been pushed together by a plow. With the aid of cooking spoons, sticks, and gloved hands, the students had tunneled into the middle. After removing snow from the center, the little hill stood firm and proud as if made of brick. The instructor had said something even more amazing: regardless how cold it got outside, the temperature inside would always stay near the freezing mark.

Standing still as stone, Travis realized that's how he knew to push snow around the shelter. He had been taught that snow was an excellent insulator. So much for memories, he mused, returning to his tasks. A little later he made another observation—the more he moved—the more the knee flexed. It still wouldn't support all his weight, but at least he didn't have to hop around everywhere on one foot.

With gear secured, Travis pulled out the compass. Map in one hand, direction finder in the other, he plotted his course. The chart showed several steep-sided hills between where he thought he might be and the hiking trail. With the bad leg, he didn't think he could climb a hill, especially in snow. The flatter route would be toward the highway. The walk would be longer, but there didn't appear to be as many ups and downs.

After filling the water bottle and stowing the pan, Travis was about ready to depart. But first he spent a few minutes using the survival tool to gouge a rope hole in the board. Once that was done, he tied the bits of twine into one longer cord. Because of the bad leg, he figured it might be easier to pull the gear than try to carry it.

Taking a last look at the dwindling fire, Travis tugged on the knot filled cord and began hobbling away—the slab of pine trailing in his tracks like a primitive tobog-gan. He paused after two dozen hard-earned steps to check the pup. It hadn't moved a muscle. The little wolf was sitting on its haunches, staring at him.

"Are you coming or not?" Travis hollered. "If we're gonna find help, we need to get going. Get over here."

The animal cocked its head, stood on three wobbly legs, and began to limp along in the boy's tracks.

* * *

The long, dark hours of night lingered on at the Larsen household much as they had for Travis. Filled with dread that their son had met with disaster, the boy's parents were far too upset to get any real rest.

Linda Larsen managed a catnap before being startled awake by a frightening dream. Just before false dawn, when the sky lightens with a promise of a new day, Roger had nodded off in the recliner. He had just drifted into a fitful slumber when he was jolted upright by the ringing of the telephone. Still half asleep, he stumbled into the kitchen a moment too late. Linda had already picked up in the bedroom. Both listened as a sheriff's deputy reviewed the earlier day's events.

"We grilled those two fellows as much as the law allows, but they stuck to their story. They claim they were only out for a recreational ski. Right! I'll believe that hogwash when pigs can fly. Anyway, they claim your boy said he was going to hike to the far end of the lake and head home from there. So here's our plan.

133

We'll keep a couple of sleds cruising up and down the original path. The remainder of the search team will focus their efforts on nearby connecting trails."

"What about the lake?" Roger blurted. "Will you be checking the lake? Trav might have broken through the ice."

"All we can do is hope for the best. The way it's snowing, there's really no way to tell. It's much too dangerous to go out on the ice. If and when the sky clears, we'll send up a helicopter, maybe a couple of search planes. Anyway, sorry to call so early, but I knew you'd be anxious to have an update."

"Yeah. You're right. We were," Roger replied. "Is it all right if I join the search team this morning?"

"Certainly. You know as much or more about the woods as any of us. That's the other reason I called. Give you a chance to pack some grub and join up with Search and Rescue. Since the fire barn burned down last month, everyone's meeting at Rollie Kane's big shed. We'll be making that headquarters until Travis is back home."

"Do you really have hopes of finding him?" Linda asked, her voice a nervous warble.

"Have faith. From what I heard about your son, it'll take more than a few snowflakes and cool breeze to stifle the lad. Best I get going. Talk to the two of you later."

"Right, and thanks," Roger said, setting the receiver into the cradle. "I hope you're right. I hope you're right."

Chapter Thirteen

CHAPTER THIRTEEN

Seth was coming down with a severe case of cabin fever. All morning he'd waited inside the cottage, hoping to hear good news. Now, in the middle of the dreary afternoon, he stood looking through the window, wondering what he could do to help.

The hours crept by on turtle feet. He'd tried taking a nap, but that didn't happen. He just tossed and turned. In his head he kept replaying the conversation overheard in the forest. Those men had to be outlaws. They certainly weren't tourists. Guys like that didn't hide snowmobiles and go for a ski without some underhanded purpose in mind.

"Sarah?" Seth said, turning to his sister. "When Mom comes back, tell her I'm out looking for Trav."

"What?" his redheaded sister blurted, glancing up from a glossy magazine. "Mom's not gonna be happy. You're gonna get in trouble."

"That's a chance I'll have to take," Seth said, pulling on winter gear. "I just can't hang around here knowing Trav is still missing. Tell mom I'll stay on the trail and be back around dark."

"Okay. I'll tell her," Sarah said. "But Seth, be careful. Going out on your own today probably isn't a good idea."

"Yeah, maybe not. But I can't stick around not knowing what's going on. Don't sweat it. I'll be fine."

"Sure, that's what you guys always say," Sarah said sarcastically. "Make sure you keep close to shore. And Seth, if you get grounded, remember I warned you."

The Polaris was once again running fine. A twist of a wrench had quickly repaired the faulty gas line connection. With fuel in the tank, and thoughts of his friend in his head, Seth pointed the machine toward the connecting trail at the end of Poplar Lake. The first thing on his agenda was to take a second look where he'd discovered the two snowmobiles.

After a fast ride, including a couple illegal shortcuts, Seth throttled the powerful sled over the road's plow ridge. He held tight to the handle-grips and directed the machine down the snowy slope. Moments later, in the murky light of a gray winter afternoon, he stepped into deep powder. The teen removed a pair of snowshoes from the carry rack. Sitting on the snowmobile seat, he attached one, then the other to his winter boots. Satisfied they were secured, he plodded into the pine grove.

The evergreens had been planted close together, and once past the perimeter, Seth stepped out of the wind. The scene was as he'd pictured. Thickly-branched trees kept snow from drifting in. And even though a half foot had fallen overnight, much of that had collected on overhead boughs. The only change was that the two men had obviously found a source for replacing the plugs. The old Skidoos were gone, but Seth could still see the depression where they'd been hidden.

"Okay," the teenage detective mumbled, pausing to take in the scene. "What exactly am I looking for?"

He stood without moving, gazing at the slight hollow where the machines had once been parked. He could see the track outline of where the men had ridden the snowmobiles through the grove and toward the highway. But there was something else. Here and there, traces of their ski path still lingered as it meandered through trees. With nothing to lose but time, Seth decided to backtrack the ski trail to see where it led.

Following tracks in the evergreens was easy. The pair had taken the most direct route from the forest and Seth effortlessly followed their path. Where the pine plantings stopped, and the mixed woods began, tracking became difficult. Out in the open woods the trail had all but disappeared. He had to stop often and study the snow, looking for any clue where the men may have passed.

He hadn't gone far when he lost the trail altogether. Being warm from walking, and frustrated at having accomplished nothing, Seth slogged to an uprooted blowdown. After clearing a spot to sit, he plopped on the tree trunk and sat pondering what to do next. His only thought was to continue along the Gunflint on the snowmobile. Maybe he could get permission from one of the rescue people to cruise the path. Decision made, he rose, swatted his backside, and began tromping around the overturned tree.

The teen wouldn't have made the find if the front of one shoe hadn't caught in a tangle of roots. One second Seth was upright, the next second he was face first in the snow. Fortunately, it was the snowshoe on his strong ankle that snagged. The unexpected tug telegraphed a searing pain up his calf. After shouting out several expletives, he wiped flakes from his face, rolled over on his back, and unbuckled the harness.

He wiggled his ankle to make sure nothing was broken or sprained. The pain was easing, and Seth sensed the

137

ache would be gone in a moment or two. Flexing the joint several times, he supported himself against the root mound and readied himself to attach the straps. He was standing alongside the hollow formed by the ripped out root system. As he bent to buckle the harness, he started to slip sideways and flung out an arm to break the fall.

At first Seth didn't know what his hand had hit—just that it was something smooth and man-made. But something smooth and man-made had no business being tucked away in a tree root. More than curious, he brushed away snow until he could tug the bag from its hiding place. As he undid the twist-tie, he exposed another sack—cream-colored—identical to the one the tall skier had attached to his packframe.

When he unsnapped the flap, Seth couldn't believe his eyes. Inside, rolled tight like a bath rug, was a thickly-furred wolf skin. At its center, wrapped in clear plastic, was the stock and barrel of a small caliber rifle. What an incredible discovery. This meant those scoundrels were not only liars, they were outlaws, and if Travis had accidentally bumped into them, he would have been in grave danger. For that matter, Seth reasoned, maybe it was already too late. Maybe the dangerous part had already taken place.

Seth shuddered at that thought, then completely ignoring the mild ache in his ankle, finished buckling the snowshoe. Scooping up the bag with both arms, he hugged it tight to his chest, and with wide duck-like steps, waddled back to the snowmobile.

Later, when arriving at the trailhead, Seth was to be disappointed. No greeting came forth from the half-dozen empty cars and pickups that filled the unplowed parking lot. He sat on the snowmobile, a bit baffled and unsure what to do next. He really didn't want to head home. After mulling over his options, he revved the engine, and despite not being asked to participate, headed toward the hiking path.

He had no idea that Search and Rescue had already scoured the first part of the trail many times over. Finding no clue Travis had recently been along that route, the group had continued the hunt well beyond Mystery Lake. They were checking all the connecting trails. If the pair of cross-country skiers had been telling the truth, Travis would have been heading to the black-top using a different route.

Seth had heard the search team discussing that possibility during the predawn briefing. He had wanted to interrupt, tell them that Travis wouldn't have changed the plan. But no, he'd been too timid; he hadn't said a word. No one asked for his opinion, and he hadn't offered it.

Deep in thought, Seth steered cautiously around each curve, angry at himself. Why hadn't he said something? Was he afraid the grown-ups wouldn't take him seriously? Or was it because deep down he wanted to be the one who brought his buddy back home? The teenager was so engaged with his own thinking, he hadn't noticed the approaching snowmobile. Looking up, he was startled to see a dark green Skidoo parked in the middle of the trail, a small cloud of bluish vapor seeping out from underneath its cowling. With only a second's hesitation, the teen veered to one side, braked, and killed the engine. After lifting the helmet visor, Seth couldn't wait to shout out the question. "Any sign of Travis?"

"Nope," came the quick reply, the rider's face partially hidden behind a smoke-colored windshield. "Who might you be? I don't recall seeing you with the others this morning. You seem a little young to be part of Search and Rescue."

"Seth. My name's Seth Springwood. Who are you?"

"Anyone know you're back here?" The stranger asked, ignoring Seth's query. "We already got one kid to be looking for. Don't need another. I suggest you turn that sled around and head back the way you came."

Annoyed by the stranger's attitude, Seth repeated his question. "I asked who you are. Do you have a name or title?"

"Seth? Is that what your name is? Best you forget about me and do as I said. Turn that big sled around and head for home. This weather ain't nothing to be out fooling around in."

"But I'm not fooling around. I need to find one of the deputies or the warden. I have some news about the men that were skiing back here."

"Yeah, is that so? What is it? You can tell me. I'll be sure to pass it along."

Seth went silent, deciding what he should say. Who knows, he reasoned, maybe this guy was in cahoots with the poachers. "That's all right," he finally stammered. "It's not all that important."

"Okay. Have it your way," came the reply. "I'll wait until you get pointed toward home and follow you out."

Seth started the engine, motored to a wide spot in the trail, and looped the snowmobile around. He was seething. Instead of being asked to help, this turkey was chasing him away. The guy can't be a local, Seth decided. Most residents along the Gunflint knew and respected the Springwoods and the Kanes. And in the two years since his dad's death, many of the neighbors had come to treat Seth as an adult, especially this past year when he had taken over much of the resort's physical work.

The creep could go climb a frozen rope, Seth fumed, gunning the engine and racing up the hill. Eyes straight ahead, he didn't slow until he reached the parking area. He pulled between a pair of pickups, slowed, and glanced over his shoulder. Just down the slope the man sat with hands gripping steering handles, a dark-visored face shield angled in Seth's direction.

"Yeah, yeah, yeah. I'm leaving," Seth mumbled behind his own face shield. "Hope your motor blows a gasket and your compass points to south." He turned the skis toward home, sat tall on the seat, and squeezed the throttle.

"What a jerk!" Seth muttered as the sled thundered up and over a hill. "What a jerk!"

* * *

"Hard work!" Travis panted. "This is really hard work!" Breaking trail in deep snow with only one good leg was more than difficult. For almost an hour he had been plodding up the grade, zigzagging between storm-snapped windfalls. But yet, when he looked behind, he could still see a bit of muted green from the big pine blowdown. Travis scowled, discouraged at his lack of progress. He hadn't traveled more than few hundred yards. Not very far for almost an hour of hard labor, he considered, especially when there might be miles yet to go.

The exertion of plunging and pushing through heavy snow more than warmed him. Travis paused to shed the parka and pack it away. Moving ahead one painful step at a time, and despite the frigid temperature, he remained hot and sweaty. After a few dozen more awkward strides, he stopped again to catch his breath. He pulled out the water bottle, took a long swig, and turned to check on the pup's progress. The wolf was close behind, sitting in the path made by the boy's oversized winter boots.

"I suppose you want some, too," Travis wheezed. "Say, how do you critters get a drink in the winter time? What d'ya do? Eat snow?"

Not expecting an answer, Travis poured a small pool into the waterproof glove as he had done the night before. Without a moment's hesitation, the thirsty animal stuck out its tongue and lapped up the offering.

"We better save some for later," the teen cautioned, straining to stand. "Too bad your leg is as useless as mine. Otherwise I'd hitch you to this toboggan and turn you into a sled dog." That said, Travis tucked the bottle away, grabbed the cord, and started moving again.

He would occasionally look up in hope that the clouds had lifted or that the snow had stopped. But nothing seemed to change. The sky remained dark and threatening—the landscape a soft white. Snowflakes, though now grainy and fine as beach sand, continued to filter through leafless branches, sometimes bullied sideways by blasts of wind.

Travis was in agony. In addition to spurts of pain from the knee, his stomach hurt and his muscles felt close to collapse. The blacktop road wouldn't be reached today. He wouldn't even get to the creek. At such a snail's pace, it could take days to find help—days he didn't have. If it would only stop snowing so he could build a smoky fire—let help come to him. But a second skyward glance confirmed that wish wasn't about to happen anytime soon.

Taking a deep breath, he plunged forward, one slow agonizing step at a time. After another half hour of painful effort, he halted, turned, and could no longer see the broken pine top. "Well, guess we made a little progress," Travis panted, clearing snow from a short section of a fallen tree.

The pup ignored the remark. Instead, the yearling had turned and stood staring into the wind. "What, you see something?" Travis asked, plopping himself down on the windfall. "Or does that shiny nose of yours smell something to eat?"

The wolf continued to gaze at their back trail, then unexpectedly lifted its head and let out a weak howl. "Sounds like you're feeling better," Travis observed, struggling upright. "But we can't stay here, pal. We gotta keep going."

Most of the afternoon hours were spent that way. Boy and animal trudging, stopping, resting, and then moving on again. Overhead, a north wind caused naked tree tops to shiver and shake—their leafless limbs bumping and punching—blocking out other sounds. Shortly before dusk Travis had no choice but to quit. The water bottle was empty, his muscles were cramping, and the knee protested every step. He had to call it a day. And before real night settled over the forest, he needed to find a place out of the wind—somewhere he could make fire.

Drained of energy, the exhausted trekker stared through the gloom, hoping to see a sheltered area. To one side the woods sloped uphill—not a good place to camp— he'd be too exposed to the elements. To his right lay a tangle of downed trees—dozens of naked branches poking up like gigantic skeletal fingers. Just beyond the clump of windfalls the ground dipped down in a soup bowl—offering a bit of protection from arctic blasts.

"Over there, Midnight," Travis wheezed. "That's where we're gonna spend some time. I don't know how you're feeling, but I've had it. We didn't get far, but at least we're closer to help than we were this morning."

It took another ten minutes of hard labor to reach the site. Once out of the wind, Travis wished he could just flop down and go to sleep. But that, he knew, might be suicidal. He might not ever wake up. His body temperature would drop like a rock from a high place. At best he'd go into the first stages of hypothermia. His thinking would become muddled and he'd make mistakes. In such wintry conditions, poor judgment just wasn't allowed.

Thick snow had drifted into the hollow. It would have to be packed before pitching the tent. Travis tugged the mask over his face, pulled on the parka, and put up the hood. He trudged to the center of the depression, sighed softly, and then flopped full length as if making a snow angel. First he rolled right, then left, and then right again. He kept moving back and forth, packing more snow on each pass. Finally satisfied there was enough space for both the shelter and a fire, he pushed himself up, grabbed the tow cord, and pulled the plank toboggan into the depression.

Now he needed to make fire. Nearby lay a large birch— its paper-thin bark curled like rolled newsprint. Travis hobbled to the limbed end and began breaking branches. The tree had been dead and leafless before falling and the branch stalks snapped with little or no effort. He pitched the fuel into the hollow, one limb at a time, until he was satisfied enough material lay scattered to temporarily feed a small blaze. Then, having planned ahead, he reached into a parka pocket. Before leaving camp that morning he had taken time to make starter material.

Travis had worried that he might be tired and cold at the end of this day. Wisely, before starting off, two pockets had been packed with dry needles and slivers of bark. Willing cold, stiff hands to work, he dragged the steel blade across the compass stone. Half a dozen strikes later, a spark settled on fluff and found a home. Hungry flames were soon gnawing their way to the larger tinder.

While Travis labored with camp work, the wolf, warm in its own winter coat, curled alongside the windfall. Twice Travis noticed the animal staring into the distance. The teenager paused and peered in the same direction. He didn't see anything unusual, only the melded gray and white of the blanketed forest.

Once the tent was set, snow was pushed up and around its sides. Even as he worked, the knee protesting every effort, Travis was aware he was losing body heat. Plugging along in the woods had been hard exercise and had kept him more than comfy. Now he wasn't moving fast enough to keep warm. Damp underclothes would have to come off.

The sleeping bag was unrolled inside the tent. Travis stripped off boots, parka, and bibs. He was right, inner clothes were soaked. As he undid the buttons of his shirt, he scented body odor. A familiar smell—the aroma the boys' locker room had after a grueling gym period. The difference, Travis mused, was that the locker room was always warm and toasty. The tent was like a meat locker. He had to hurry.

The turtleneck top was damp—as if removed mid-cycle from a clothes dryer. Travis paused, shivering on his knees, wondering how he could dry things. It had to be done. Wet fabric stole heat and he had none to spare.

What had he read in survival books? He didn't think the fire was the answer. With wind, it would be nearly impossible to get garments close enough without scorching. An immediate choice had to be made, because dressed only in T-shirt and briefs, he was beginning to shiver violently. He couldn't wait any longer. With a sudden burst of movement, he opened the sleeping bag and slid inside. The clothes would have to freeze themselves dry. Travis curled up in the bag, hugging himself, and after long moments, the shaking slowed.

From outside the tent came a pitiful whine. Having been so miserable, Travis had neglected his traveling companion. And though exhausted, he thought it best to bring the pup inside. Forcing himself to move, Travis managed to squirm the bag close to the door. With one arm exposed, he worked the zipper open and called to the young predator. "Come on, Midnight. It's warmer in here. Come on boy."

Not wanting to leave the sleeping sack, but knowing he had to, Travis slithered out into the cold air. He threw the hood of the parka over his head, not bothering to put his arms through the sleeves. Sitting on the bag, and with every movement coming at a cost, he pulled on his boots. Then, while crawling out of the tent, he again called for the pup. "Come on, wolf. Get over here."

Can't expect a wild critter to know commands, Travis reasoned, wiggling more into the open. Looking up, he almost swallowed his tongue. Sitting on haunches, near the branched end of a slender birch windfall, were three mature timber wolves, each half again the size of the yearling.

Travis froze, half in, half out of the shelter. The large meat-eaters sat mute, looking his way. After a long moment Travis cast his eyes down. The pup was standing on the far side of the fire, also peering at the uninvited visitors. Unexpectedly, the yearling lifted its head and let out a pitiful yelp.

The unexpected cry startled Travis, and with all his weight on one knee, caused him to lose balance. His arms were tucked inside the jacket, hands clutching the zippered sides. Unable to stop, he tipped over. For a brief moment he lay still, then remembering his terror, pushed up. He wiped snow from his face, looked at the pup, and then turned toward the wolves. Gone—vanished. In only the few seconds he had been struggling in the snow, the predators had disappeared.

Had he imagined them? Was his mind playing tricks? Knowing he wouldn't sleep until he knew for certain, Travis pulled a thick branch from the fire pile. With heart thumping, and staying in the footprints from wood-gathering, he limped to the end of the windfall.

No. He hadn't imagined anything. The tracks didn't lie. Three depressions waited for his inspection. And three sets of prints joined into one narrow trail leading up and over the rise. Terror-struck, Travis was oblivious that he was standing half-naked in the biting wind. Didn't he have enough problems without worrying about a pack of wolves? His bare legs started to shiver, jerking him back to reality.

He limped to the fire, and after adding more fuel, stood close, toasting goose-bumped skin and considering nightfall. He was unlucky enough to be hurt, cold, and famished, without having a new worry. Would the wolves return? And if they did, would they attack? Were they as hungry as he was?

When his legs warmed, Travis returned to the tent. He tried coaxing the pup to join him, but the animal ignored the invitation. It was curled in the snow, content to stay outside. Was the wild dog trying to make a decision? Probably. No doubt it wants to follow its family. With that guess in mind, Travis slid into the tent, zipped the door tight, and returned to the relative comfort of the sleeping bag.

"Might be the last night of my life," Travis mumbled through chattering teeth. "Might be my last night." The exhausted teenager pulled the bag over his head, curled into a ball, and hoped sleep would come soon.

Chapter Fourteen

C H A P T E R   F O U R T E E N

Travis awoke cold and confused. Like an ice chest with its lid tightly in place, the inside of the tent was an inky black, and just about as frigid. It took Travis a moment or two to become fully alert. When cobwebs cleared, the teen realized he was shaking violently. He wrapped his arms around his chest and tucked hands into his armpits. Even his fingers felt thick and clumsy, as if they'd been borrowed from a stranger. Then he forced himself to rock back and forth until the shivering slowed and he could collect his thoughts. "Fire and food. I need fire and food," he mumbled, forcing himself to slither out of the bag. "I'd better be up to the fire part."

Travis reached for his turtleneck and winter underwear. The turtleneck felt stiff—wooden—frozen hard as a board. The long johns, though frigid, were more flexible. Unlike the cotton top, the fabric was of man-made material, designed not to absorb much in the way of moisture.

With painstaking effort, he managed to get his legs into the waistband of the underwear. Not until he had tugged the bottoms into place did he notice they were on backwards. He cursed at his carelessness. They'd have to stay that way—it was too cold to switch. Lying on his back, he slid into the bibs, and then sat up to put on his shirt and parka. For a few anxious moments he couldn't find the boots. Flopping onto his stomach, he swept his arms out in concern. Relief—cold fingers found one, then the other.

After a brief battle with the zippered door, Travis crawled outside, hopeful that a bit of the earlier blaze still clung to life. No such luck. Where the fire should have been was now a dusky hollow surrounded by chalky white. He inched forward on all fours to the dark depression. Grasping the unburned end of a fire spoke in a gloved hand, he poked at the shadow, expecting to find a hot ember or two. All hope evapo-rated as he stirred through the meager ash pile. Nothing. Not even a spark.

Using the partially burned branch for support, Travis pushed upright. Could he make fire in the dark? In snow? With cold and clumsy fingers? Probably not. And why bother? If the fire wasn't fed every hour, it'd starve and be dead and cold by morning. He'd just have to survive the night without heat. At first light, when he could see what he was doing, he could try. But not now, it was too dark, and his fingers were too stiff.

What the cold camper wanted was to crawl into the tent, slip into the bag, drift off to sleep. But he was still thinking clearly enough to realize that might be committing suicide. Arms and legs already wanted to shut down. Without fire, there was only one cure— he had to get his blood pumping. The only answer was to exercise.

He began circling the shelter. At first the knee disap-proved of every step. But by the time he'd made a dozen laps, the walking became less of a chore. His wide winter boots took on the task of packing snow and soon he could almost shuffle—easing the effort on the injured limb.

He limped and limped around the tent—when it suddenly dawned on him—he hadn't seen the pup. Travis hobbled to where the wolf had bedded near the birch. Even in the dark, the glossy black coat should have been an easy mark on the bleached background. But like the search for hot coals in cold ashes—there was nothing to see. The only hint to where the yearling slept was a slight dent in the snow.

Puzzled, Travis dropped on his good knee, patted the hollow, and felt his despair deepen. A half-inch of new powder covered the wolf's bed and he couldn't help feeling a bit abandoned. Cold, weary, and depressed, Travis limped back to the tent and began circling again. Once warmed, he could think about crawling back in the bag. And when he did, regardless of what he'd read in books, he'd be wearing every stitch of clothing he had brought along on the trip.

* * *

The beam of the snowmobile headlight sliced through the gloom of early evening. Seth was navigating on autopilot, wrapped up in his own thoughts. Whom should he tell about the sack of evidence tied tight in the carry rack? And what excuse was he going to give to his mother for going out on his own?

Seth came out of his musings not certain of his surroundings. He'd been squeezing the throttle in such a mental fog that he'd paid no mind to trail markings. Luckily, the headlamp reflected off a sign pointing toward Poplar Lake. Feeling a sense of relief, he let off the gas, and swung the machine in the direction of the arrow.

The decision was made while the snowmobile was humming along the lake's edge. He'd tell Doug Davis, his mother's fiancé. A widower himself, Doug had come on the scene during the fall outing. He'd helped transport Seth out of the storm-twisted forest. Since then,

150

the Springwoods had seen a great deal of the man. And Seth was certain he'd be seeing a lot more of the man in the future, as Seth's mother was busy making plans for a June wedding.

Seth chose not to park the snowmobile in the storage shed. Instead, when he reached the resort beach, he turned, drove up the bank, and plowed a path to the cabin's back step. Two vehicles cowered in the blustering wind. The Ford pickup his mother often used to transport resort supplies rested near the entry door. Parked alongside the old truck was Doug Davis' dark green SUV, snowflakes melting on a warm hood.

Switching the key off, Seth hesitated, wondering how to explain his find to the adults inside. After a moment of uncertainty, he decided to tell everything just as it had happened. His mother would be upset to hear that he'd been roaming about on his own. So be it. He couldn't help that. Finding Travis was more important than getting a lecture or being grounded.

After removing his helmet, Seth clomped up the snow-covered steps. He paused at the door, stealing a look inside. Sarah and Doug sat across from each other at the dining room table, chatting. His mother had her back to him—clutching the telephone to her ear.

Seth mentally braced himself, stomped snow from his boots, and turned the knob. As he stepped in, he was greeted by a rush of warm air and the scent of biscuits baking in the oven. The clunk of the door closing caused his mother to turn and stare. Sarah and Mr. Davis stopped in mid-sentence to do the same. Letting out an exasperated sigh, Mrs. Springwood apologized to whoever was on the other end of the conversation. "You were right. He just walked in. Sorry to have bothered you."

Seth knelt and started unlacing his boots. He cleared his throat, and without looking at anyone in particular, gave a short speech. "Hope you're not mad. It got dark sooner than I thought."

For a moment his mother said nothing. When she spoke, the relief in her voice was obvious. "Seth, I don't know if I should hug you or ground you. How could you go off by yourself, especially with Travis missing? I swear, you buzzing about who knows where is going to turn my hair gray."

"Jeez, Mom, it's no big deal. I never went far from the highway. I had to do something. I'm the one who dropped Trav off, remember?"

"Remember? How can I forget? By now everyone up and down the Gunflint knows about Travis. Then, when I come home and Sarah tells me you went off by yourself, I about had a heart attack."

Neither Doug nor Sarah said a word, but Sarah gave Seth a look that said, 'I told you so.' Mr. Davis appeared to want to say something, but not yet being the step-father, thought better of it.

"Okay, okay. I should have had someone ride along. But I'm fine, see?" Seth answered, standing tall and turning around like a model for inspection. "I think I did good. I didn't see any sign of Trav, but I do know those two characters' story was a bunch of baloney."

"Really? What d'ya find? Anything to help Search and Rescue?" Mr. Davis asked in his deep voice.

"I'm not exactly sure. But I do know those two creeps fibbed to the cops," Seth answered, giving his mother a pleading smile.

When Seth finished recounting the afternoon adventure, including the part about the rude man he met on the trail, a hush fell over the cabin. The only sound came from an antique grandfather clock 'tick-tocking' in a distant corner. Mr. Davis broke the interlude.

"Seth, after we eat, you and I should take your discovery down to the shed. One of the deputies should be there waiting for others to return."

He focused on Seth's mother for agreement. "I think you might be right. For now, the fewer people who know about your find, the better. For all we know, someone local might be in cahoots with those characters you ran into."

Mr. Davis again looked at his soon-to-be bride, making direct eye contact. "What do you think, Lynn? Is it all right if Seth and I go out for a little while?"

Lynn Springwood gazed lovingly at her son—anger having been replaced with relief. "Of course," she answered, walking over to her offspring and giving him a hug around the shoulders. "As long as he stays with you, I'll know he's safe. Now let's eat."

Later, his stomach full, his feet warmed, Seth bundled up for the short trip to the garage. He was to return the snowmobile to the shed while Mr. Davis drove the SUV around on the driveway. They were hoping none of the volunteers were in the building. They wanted to transfer the garbage sack, and information that went with it, to someone with a title or badge.

A few minutes later Seth parked the Polaris and waited to be let into the building. Wind-driven snow swept off the lake and swirled around the shed. The wide wooden door swung up with a sudden burst. Doug Davis stood grasping the bottom in one hand, gesturing to Seth with the other.

Without delay, the teen motored the machine inside and the door quickly closed behind him. It took a moment for the boy's eyes to adjust to the bright light. When he could see clearly, Seth realized they weren't alone. Two men were sitting on folding chairs in front of a portable heater.

Without any introduction, one of the men spoke up. "See you made it home okay. Why didn't you tell me you were from the resort? I wouldn't have been so quick to turn you around."

Seth gave Mr. Davis a questioning look before answering. "No problem. I needed to get home anyway. It got dark sooner than I thought. My mom was pretty worried."

The second man stood and strolled to the Polaris. With a gloved hand he poked a finger at the bag bundled in the carrier. "What's in the sack? You been out doing some roadside cleanup?"

Seth eyed Mr. Davis, this time for help. Doug caught the clue and moved to the rear of the machine. "This?" Doug said. "It's nothing. Just some extra clothes Seth brought along in case he found his friend."

With a sweep of an arm, Mr. Davis plucked the package in one hand and swung it over his shoulder. "Seth, I'll put the bag in my car. I'll drop it off at the cottage later."

Seth was quick to reply. "Thanks. My mom doesn't know I took her snowmobile gear from the closet. Best if I just sneak it back in."

The bag-poker seemed satisfied. He turned to the first man. "What time do you think the others will be here? I need to get to town, got a couple of errands to run. Way it's comin' down, it'll be a slow drive."

"Who knows? Soon, I should think. Not much anyone can do in the dark. You got things to do, go ahead, take off. I suspect everyone will meet here before first light in the morning."

"Yeah, okay. I think I'll go. If it doesn't snow all night, I'll be here 'bout an hour before sunrise." Without another word, the man turned and exited through the side door.

Seth sat on the snowmobile, waiting for Mr. Davis to speak. The teen didn't want to say anything in front of the second stranger. Studying the man closely, Seth realized this was the same guy who had treated him so rudely on the trail.

"You're Doug Davis, right?" the man inquired, rising from his folding chair.

"Yep, I am," Mr. Davis answered with a hint of caution in his voice. "And just who might you be?"

"Name's Higgins. Sheriff told me about you. Says you can be counted on to keep a secret. Does that hold true with you, too, Seth?"

The youth didn't know what to say. The man seemed different now. His voice was pleasant—not threatening as it been earlier. "Maybe, if I know the reason. But right now I haven't the slightest clue as to why I should," Seth replied, switching his eyes back and forth between the two adults.

"I can respect that," the stranger said, digging into a pocket. He pulled out his wallet and continued, "I'm only showing you this because I think you know more than you let on earlier. About that garbage sack, what's really in there? You find something I should know about?"

The stranger eased to where Seth slouched on the snowmobile. He flipped open his wallet to display a fancy badge and ID photo. "Actually my title is Special Agent Higgins. I'm a wildlife warden working under-cover. Part of my job is to help local officials handle poaching problems—particularly those involving endangered or threatened species."

The man looked directly at the teenager before continu-ing. "And I'm sorry to have been so impolite to you out on the trail. I was just trying to keep my cover a secret. Only the deputies and the warden know my true identity. Search and Rescue volunteers were told that I'm a fur buyer from the cities and just happened to be in the area for a few days of snowmobiling."

Seth took the wallet from the man's hand and studied it, not knowing what to look for. He passed the wallet to Mr. Davis. "What do you think? Is it real?"

Mr. Davis took a moment before answering. "Yeah, I believe it is. Nice to meet you," Doug said, extending his hand. "I think we have something you'll want to see."

Mr. Davis and Agent Higgins were about to leave when Rollie Kane suddenly burst through the side entry door, ushered in by a blast of frosty air. "Blazes! Don't get winter weather for weeks, then 'ka-bam!' it comes all at once!" the rosy-cheeked man declared to no one in particular.

"Oh! There you are. I was getting worried about you," Rollie said, turning his fogged-covered glasses in Seth's direction. "With the wind whipping off the lake, it ain't fit for man nor beast outside. Glad to see you had enough sense to come in where it's warm. So tell me: what d'ya find on your expedition? Any sign of your bud?"

Seth glanced over at the others, wondering how much he could say. Higgins read the question in the youth's eyes and answered for him. "Mr. Kane, you don't know me, but I've heard about you."

"Is that so, young feller? All good, I hope," Rollie replied, studying the stranger through hazy bifocals.

"Yep, as a matter of fact, it is. I know that you've lived along the Trail for many years and that you also have a reputation as a square shooter."

"What d'ya mean by that? A square shooter?" Rollie asked, pulling out a large handkerchief and proceeding to wipe his round, pink-tinted nose.

"I mean you're someone who can be trusted to keep a secret, like Mr. Davis here. And, of course, your young business partner," he added, giving Seth a nod of his head.

"Of course I can keep a secret. What's on your mind?"

Higgins explained who he was and why he was involved. Rollie kept quiet, letting the stranger go on in detail. When Higgins finished, the resort keeper was quiet, the fingers of one hand unconsciously stroking his beard.

After a long pause, he spoke in a voice that was all business. "Okay, see if I've got this straight. You think there's a poaching gang 'round here. And you think who's ever doing the killing is primarily after wolf hair. I hate to hear that's happening, but I'm not certain how I can be of any help."

"Well, since you seem to know just about everyone in the area, I'd like to pick your brain. See who we should take a closer look at. Maybe whoever's involved has a contact along the Trail—someone you're familiar with."

"Be glad to give you any information I can. But pickin' my brain, young man, is a little like gnawing on a bleached bone—there's not a whole lot left to offer. Off the top of my head, I can't think of a single person," Rollie said, thought furrows creasing his ruddy forehead.

He paused, then let out a sigh before continuing. "So you think there's a connection between those two rascals Seth ran across the other day and Travis' disappearance? Is that where you're going?"

With a shrug of his shoulders and a nod of his head, Higgins agreed. "Don't see it any other way. I think Travis came across those two by accident. Once they were discovered, they had no choice but to lose the boy."

"What d'ya mean, 'lose the boy?'" Rollie interrupted, eyes wide with amazement.

157

"I mean, I don't think they would have injured Travis. Those characters aren't people killers. They're just a couple of two-bit sneak thieves. They'd think nothing of picking your pocket or shooting an animal in or out of season. But I don't think they'd chance murder."

For the first time since Rollie had arrived, Doug Davis shared an opinion. "What we think, Rollie, is that they took Travis off the trail. Probably heisted his food, hope he gets lost. The way these guys think, it'd be ruled an accident. Young fellow goes out on his own, gets caught in a storm, dies, and the body is never found. In their twisted minds, something like that wouldn't be the same as killing a kid outright."

Rollie shook his head and drew in a deep breath, processing the reality of what he had just been told. "That means Travis might be alive. Cold, hungry, scared out of his wits, but alive. Is that what you think?"

"Very possible," Doug answered. "Travis learned a lot when he was trapped by the autumn storm. We talked about it. The most important thing he learned was never to panic and to take one step at a time. If I remember correctly, he even taught himself how to make fire without matches."

Hearing these words from a skilled outdoorsman, Seth felt a small ray of hope. Maybe his buddy was okay. Maybe, when the snow stopped, Travis would walk out without help.

"Let's keep this under our hats for now," Higgins said. "Rollie, I'll get one of the deputies to meet with us before the others arrive in the morning. Until then, try to think of anyone in the area who might be a silent partner to the poachers. Meantime, let's pray that the Larsen boy is out of the wind and tucked in his bag for the night."

"Got it," Rollie agreed. "I'll also ask for the snow to stop. Seth, try to get some rest. There's nothing more you can do tonight."

"Come on, young man," Mr. Davis urged. "Let's go to the cabin and catch some shut-eye. I have a feeling tomorrow's going to be another long day."

"Good idea. I'll go out with you. You have a sack I need to sneak into my truck," Higgins said, heading for the door. "See you 'bout six in the a.m., Mr. Kane. And you get some sleep, too. We all need to be sharp come morning."

Chapter Fifteen

C H A P T E R   F I F T E E N

Travis couldn't take another step. He'd lost track of how many times he'd trudged around the little tent. The knee was throbbing, his stomach ached, and his mouth was dry as a cotton ball. But he felt warmer.

He exhaled a deep burst of air, his open mouth puffing like a small steam engine, and wondered if he had enough energy to rekindle the fire. To do that, he'd have to venture from camp in search of more tinder. Probably best to try now, he decided. Come morning, his muscles and limbs would be stiff and shivery, maybe even too numb to make the effort.

Removing a mitten, Travis dug in the pockets of the bibs, hoping to find a few errant scraps of tinder. Fingers brushed the corners of the right pocket— empty. But hiding in the bottom of the left pocket—success. Now he only needed a few dry twigs. He shuffled along the big birch blowdown, snapped snippets of thin, barren limbs, and stuffed pockets until they were packed.

At the fire site he used his boot to brush away snow. Kneeling, he emptied his pockets, pulled out the compass, and then stopped. Gazing up, grainy flakes of snow stinging his eyes, he began to pray. "God, I don't know why you keep testing me. I always try to do the right thing. I try to follow the rules. So if you're listening, please let me start this fire. 'Cause God, I'm scared. I don't want to die. Please, you gotta help me."

His words were swallowed by the wind and swept into the forest. But by having said the prayer, Travis felt a sense of calm. He'd try to make fire, and if he didn't prevail, he'd crawl back in the bag and hope for the best. The situation was becoming more than he could deal with. There was only a slim winter chance that he'd be able to save himself.

Travis was about to form the fire nest when he remembered the flashlight. It was tucked in the top pocket of the pack. He'd wanted to save the batteries in case he needed to signal and hadn't used it much. But light might help him start a fire. If he didn't build the nest correctly, he probably wouldn't be alive long enough to use the beam as a signaling beacon.

The anemic stream of light proved useful. In less than a minute a small twig tepee had been assembled. Then, positioning his body to block the wind, Travis said a silent prayer, and ripped the tip of the rough blade across the strip of gray material. Once, twice, three times, he pitted steel against stone. Zilch. Not a single spark emerged.

Anxious, he let the little rubber handled flashlight drop from his mouth. Settling into the snow, its beam became a weak yellow candle. Fingers were growing numb. If he was to make fire, he'd have to do it now or forget about it altogether.

Scrunching even closer, Travis dragged the blade across the flint. This time sparks flashed. Stupid, stupid, he scolded himself. The sparks were there before, but because of the light, he hadn't been able to see them.

Again he struck stone. A miniature meteor shower leapt from the compass cover and nestled on fluff. Oblivious to the throbbing knee, Travis knelt with his face only inches away, took a breath, and blew a steady stream of air. The magic took place; his prayer was answered. The fuzz burst into flame. He could breathe a little easier. Once flames were bright enough to broadcast a peach-colored working light, Travis tugged the sleeping bag from the tent and placed it near the heat. With a spurt of extra effort, he'd bullied through snow some fifty feet to a small spruce. The tree's frozen boughs, stiff and brittle as glass, snapped easily in mitten covered hands. When a half-dozen needled shoots lay at his feet, he gathered them to his chest and trudged the whole bundle back to camp.

Since the autumn storm's close call, Travis had scoured every outdoor education book in the town library. He recalled reading that spruce trees could be a winter survivor's last chance. The thickly needled branches had two uses. The first purpose was fairly obvious. Spruce boughs made excellent insulation.

The second use was nutritional. One text claimed a starving winter camper should consider making spruce needle tea. The tea itself would yield a bit of nourishment, and the warm brew would help refill the body's lack of liquid. With the fire burning with noisy pops and snaps, Travis dug out the cooking pot and packed it full of clean snow.

Next, he pulled three forked branches from the wood supply, rigged a simple tripod, and hung the small kettle over the fire. That done, all he could do now was wait. After brushing snow from his bibs and boots, and fully dressed, he slipped into the sleeping bag.

The fire, parka, vest, and bed of spruce boughs made a huge difference. Inside the bag, close to the blaze, Travis was almost comfortable. But he didn't dare doze off. He had to keep the fire burning and finish brewing tea. His body needed fluids. His stomach craved something—anything—to fill the empty void.

Travis had to slide in and out of the bag a half-dozen times. As snow warmed and turned to melt, the pot needed to be repacked. When the pan was finally half full of water, he began stripping needles from a healthy looking branch. These he sprinkled into the steaming liquid, making the water rise. With needles and water filling the pot to the brim, he replaced the kettle over the fire.

Then he knelt to the side, steadying the pot with a stick, not wanting the contents to spill. At last the water began boiling, a cloud of steam teaming with wood smoke before being whisked away by the breeze. Travis stirred and stirred, willing the short green needles to give up their vitamins and minerals.

How long, he pondered, does one brew a pot full of needles? Then a second thought. How do you drink a steaming liquid filled with hundreds of tiny tree parts? He mused about that for a moment before an idea took shape. The face mask. Pull the fabric over his mouth, use the material as a filter, and slowly sip the strange soup.

He held back, waiting for the tea to cool. When he could hold the pot without burning bare fingers, he brought the liquid up to fabric covered lips. It was unlike anything he'd ever tasted. Bitter, piney, and nothing like the real thing. Travis paused until his stomach gurgled, reminding him that for days little had passed its way. He lifted the pan to his lips and took a second sip. Drop by drop, the warm fluid trickled through fabric and eased down his throat.

Too soon the strange drink disappeared. All that remained was a heap of soggy needles clumped together at the bottom of the pan. And though the tea tasted terrible, it helped fill his belly. He wanted more.

By soft fire light, shadows mimicking every move, Travis made another pot. And still a third time, until his stomach felt full.

The blazing fire had gnawed deeply into the fuel supply. The weary camper hobbled to the birch and began twisting and snapping limbs. But the bizarre brew had worked. He felt a little better—had a bit more energy. Though bone tired, he could function. With a small stack of wood piled, the fire feeding itself, his belly sloshing, Travis finally dared to rest. After tucking himself inside the bag, he pulled the cover over his head, and immediately fell asleep.

Soon after the first snore, thick cold flakes, twisting and dancing to gusts of arctic air, once again began collecting on the forest floor. Old Man Winter refused to call it a night, and like long distance runner, had just gotten a second wind.

* * *

The state of mind at the Larsen household was one of dread and worry. Soon after Agent Higgins had departed, Mr. Davis had phoned Roger. He filled in the details of Seth's discovery. Then he explained to Mr. Larsen the theory they had developed, that the poachers may have forced Travis deep into the forest, taken his supplies, and left him to find his way out. Finished relating the events, Doug inquired if Roger wanted to meet before the others arrived in the morning. The answer was a definite 'yes.'

Linda Larsen was a bundle of nervous energy. For the second time in three months her first born was missing—presumed dead. She was furious at herself for not putting her foot down—just saying no to the trip. If and when Travis returned, she wouldn't let the boy out of her sight until he was ready to leave for college.

Travis' younger sister, Beth, was equally agitated. Things had just returned to normal, and once again, her big brother was missing. When the ten-year-old wasn't busy answering the phone, she stood staring out the window, willing the snow to stop.

* * *

Seth couldn't come awake. He was in the middle of a dream but something kept bumping his shoulder. The thumping on his arm continued, followed by a voice. "Seth, wake up. It's time to go."

"Huh?" The teen managed to mumble, still in a foggy state of sleep. "Go away. I'm tired."

"Seth. It's Doug. Wake up. We need to get an early start."

"Hmm…you go ahead without me," came the muffled reply from under the pillow.

"You sure? You can stay home if you like. Go out later with the snowmobile."

There was a moment of silence as Seth tried to clear his head. In a sleep-filled whisper he said, "Yeah. I'll do that. I'll ride up there a little later on the Polaris."

"Okay. But if you do go out, make sure you stay on the trail. And Seth."

"Huh?" Seth yawned.

"Make sure you pack along some snacks and matches, just in case."

"Yeah. Okay, I'll see you later. Just need a few minutes to wake up." With those words, the drowsy teenager rolled over and closed his eyes.

Later, as soft light filtered through the bedroom window, Seth bolted upright with the sudden realization he'd overslept. From under the door came the scent of frying bacon, urging him to get a move on. After a quick visit to the bathroom, he stumbled into the living area.

Across the pine-paneled room, his mother was working at the stove. Not fully alert, Seth leaned against the door frame wearing only a T-shirt and briefs. He realized his mistake too late. His mom turned and flashed a small smile. "Good morning. I thought you could use a good breakfast before you start shoveling."

"Shoveling? Aah Mom…I don't have time to shovel. I have to meet Doug at the trailhead. I said I'd be up there right after first light."

"No, I don't think so. Let Search and Rescue do their job. I'd like for you stay around the resort this morning. More snow came down while you were in bed. We're about snowed in. You can help Rollie clear the paths and parking areas. Maybe he'll even let you drive the old plow truck."

Any other time Seth would have jumped at the chance to operate the ancient pickup used to clear the drive. Not now. He had only one thing on his mind. "Cripes, Mom. I can do the snow when I come home. I need to make another run up that trail Travis used. I don't think the rescue people are looking in the right places."

His mother set the spoon down, paused, and then walked across the room. Seth was trapped, wishing he had taken time to dress. As she came closer, he noticed she'd been crying. Her usually clear blue eyes were rimmed with red and a wad of tissue was stuffed in the pocket of her robe.

She stopped, raised her hands to his shoulders, and took a long, deep breath. "Honey, I know how you must be feeling. Helpless, confused, worried. We all are. But I just can't stand the thought of you winding up like Travis."

Seth felt a surge of shock, waking him to full attention. "Mom, Travis is okay. Sure, he's been gone for a few days, but he's okay. I know he is."

Squeezing his shoulders, she sounded close to tears. "Oh Seth, I hope so. I so hope you're right. We all do. I don't know how Linda and Roger can stand going through this a second time."

She was quiet for a moment, her gaze directed at a spot over Seth's shoulder. Then in almost a whisper, she asked, "Do you know how much I worry when you take off on that snowmobile? I wish those darn things had never been invented. Seth, I'd never forgive myself if I let you go out in this storm and something dreadful happened."

"Mom, I'm almost fifteen. I can take care of myself. Besides, there'll be plenty of others around today. 'Cause Mom, I gotta go. I gotta help find Trav. He's like family and I know he'd be looking for me if things were reversed."

Lynn Springwood removed her hands from her son's shoulders, and before Seth could escape, gave the boy a big hug. Just as quickly she released him, turned and went back to the stove. The bacon was beginning to burn.

"I know, Seth. I know. Go. But be careful. And please, try to be home before dark."

* * *

Travis awoke in a state of panic. It took a moment to chase away the cobwebs—to remember he was tucked inside a sleeping sack—far from home. The bag's normally light weight fabric weighed heavily against him and he realized it must be covered with drifted snow. He lay shivering, wondering if that's what awakened him, when something bumped his foot. Once, twice, three times. Alarm bells went off in his head. An animal was on the outside—trying to paw its way to the inside.

The digging stopped, and in the deafening silence that followed, Travis heard a muffled whimper. Then the pawing began again. Terrified, Travis lay frozen with fear, certain he was about to become a meal.

The scratching ceased only to be followed by a soft whine. Recognition buzzed through the boy's brain. He knew that sound. It was the same whimper he'd heard when he had placed the yearling on the drag. Travis managed to wiggle his head back and forth to gain space enough to speak. "Midnight? Is that you?"

The only reply was more digging. Like a frozen pipe thawing, warm relief began to trickle through the teen. It had to be the wolf pup. What else could it be? Other animals would have backed away from the sound of his voice.

Still a bit nervous, Travis lay quiet, considering his next move. The pawing continued, accompanied by more whining. Enough proof. There was nothing to fear. Slipping his arms over his head, Travis attempted to sit up. Impossible. The weight of the snow had pinned him to the ground.

This was one of the youth's worst fears. He absolutely could not stand tight, closed spaces. To think he might be buried under a snow drift was more than he could tolerate. Without thought, and in full alarm, Travis began battling the bag. He twisted and turned, bucked and jerked—the fear complete—his body moving without reason or plan.

Suddenly, like pushing through a trap door, he popped free. With more shifting and shaking, he was able to sit up. But the struggling didn't stop until he was completely upright. Then, as quickly as the wild dance had begun, it was over. Travis stood like a department store mannequin—trying to calm his thoughts—trying to catch his breath.

The first light of morning, dull and dreary, was just beginning to seep into the forest. A good half-foot of snow had fallen overnight—adding yet another layer to the landscape—thickening the wooly, winter coat. At first Travis didn't notice the yearling. The wolf had backed away when the teen had started jerking about. Now it stood some twenty feet distant—eyes steady—studying the human. Travis also stared, surprised, but happy, that his wilderness friend had returned.

After a moment or two, Travis found his voice. "Good morning. Glad to have you back. Did you happen to bring breakfast?"

The animal stood mute. Then, one small step at a time, inched forward. When it was several feet away, it stopped, looked up, and whimpered.

"What? Are you trying to tell me something?" Travis stammered through chattering teeth. "I don't speak wolf. And guess what? I don't have anything for you to eat either."

Another moment passed, neither making a sound. Travis began to shiver. The warmth created by the burst of activity was quickly evaporating. He had to either exercise or kindle a fire. Turning his back to the animal, he inspected the sleeping bag. It lay partially buried in the snow—its outer shell changed from deep blue to wedding cake white.

Travis bent, grabbed the bag with both hands, and shook it clean. Then he folded the bag over an arm and turned toward the shelter. The tent had all but disappeared. Though it was just a few feet away, only a snowy mound gave clue to its presence.

Moving away from the previously packed fire pit area gave Travis new alarm. With another half foot added to the quilt, the snow was now more than knee deep. Once again he felt familiar stirrings in the pit of his stomach. Frustrated, filled with fear, and not knowing what else to do, he turned his face skyward, raised an arm, and shook his fist. "You're gonna let me die, aren't you! You're really gonna let me die!"

Muffled by the mantled forest, the words had a quick death. Trembling, Travis fell to his knees, chest wrenching, eyes wet and unfocused. He stayed hunched over, sobbing, until there were no more tears to shed. When at last he looked up, he was surprised to see the wolf standing close. The animal's face was tipped to one side as if asking what the fuss was about.

"Okay, okay," Travis sighed. "So I've got a problem, a real doozy of a problem. But I'm still alive, I'm still able to think. I'm still able to move. I'll figure out a way to get out of here. But first, let's see if I can get a fire going."

By probing around the fire circle he located a half-dozen unburned limbs. He used one to stir the ashes. Success—a small miracle. Napping deep in the pile of cinders were three live coals. Without delay, Travis whittled wood shavings from a branch. He carefully placed the tinder on the embers, knelt, and blew. Several breaths later the paper-thin kindling smoked, glowed red, and burst into flames.

Once the fire was burning on its own, Travis turned his attention to the tent. He discovered he could move about if he stayed on the firmly packed paths from the previous day's chores. There he only had to plow through the six inches of overnight fluff.

Working vigorously, ignoring hunger pains, he cleared the tent's entrance—all the while forming a plan. One way or another, the snowshoes would have to be repaired. There was no time to waste. It had to be done this morning. He had to make his escape today.

In another day or two he wouldn't have the strength to make it out on his own. The only chance was to somehow secure a fix, because without snowshoes, he had no way out.

How, and with what, could repairs be made? He pondered that question over and over as he dug in the snow for the pine board. The first mending efforts using birch branches hadn't worked. Besides, there wasn't nearly enough binding rope.

"Whoa! Wait a minute!" Travis announced to the white world around him. "Underwear! My underwear! I can use my long johns! They're tougher than nails, and once I'm walking, I won't need them. My bibs are more than enough to keep me warm."

Stripping to bare-bottom skin would prove to be one of the hardest parts of the project. The first step was pushing the plank flat on the snow. He opened the sleeping bag over the board, and then raced to remove boots and outer clothing. By the time he'd stripped off the bottoms, he was shivering violently.

With clenched jaw and jerky movements, he managed to pull on the bibs. Then after slipping his feet into his boots, he leaned close to the fire, savored its warmth, and waited for the shaking to subside. Stuffing himself into vest and parka was a breeze. As each layer of clothing went on, he felt his body heat return, and almost as if he'd stepped inside a building, the shivering came to an end.

After a few trips to a windfall gathering fuel, Travis was almost warm. He stood near the heat and mulled over what to do next. During the hectic activity he'd hadn't paid any attention to the wolf. Now, as he looked about the campsite, he couldn't see the animal. Moving closer to the tent, he spotted fresh tracks meandering off into the forest; a major disappointment. He was hoping the yearling would stay near camp, would keep him company. But he didn't have time to dwell on regrets. If he was going to save himself, he had things to do. He had to get to work.

The first thing was to set the pot over the fire. He needed a full water bottle. If he was to be hiking on snowshoes, he'd need lots of liquid. Once he prepared the cooking pot, he brushed snow from the plank, and eased himself into a sitting position.

Using the smaller of the survival tool's two razor-edged blades, Travis began cutting the long johns into strips. The first ribbon was several inches wide. He tested its strength by wrapping each end around a hand and pulling. The fabric stretched, but showed no sign of ripping. He cut the next sample thinner and gave it the same exam. The fabric refused to break. Satisfied the material could be cut into even narrower sections, the teen worked nonstop slicing and ripping.

Except to warm his hands, and occasionally refill the pot, Travis labored without a break. When only the waist band remained, dozens of fabric ribbons rested atop the plank.

Reaching into the tent, he slid out the packframe, snowshoes and all. Then sitting alongside the fire, a splintered shoe on his lap, Travis suddenly felt stupid. The wood he needed for the repair was all around camp. Several nearby tipped-over spruce trees had branches of every size and length. Spruce boughs were springy and tough, and would work much better than brittle birch limbs. And with so many fabric ties, there should be more than enough material to wrap and bind all the outer edges.

Eager to get started, Travis hobbled to the end of the largest windfall. The very top boughs were new growth from the past summer season. They'd be flexible and sturdy, perfect for what he had in mind. He opened the survival tool and went to work. Maybe there was still a cold chance he could save himself. The odds weren't great, but it was the only opportunity he'd get.

Chapter Sixteen

CHAPTER SIXTEEN

Seth was upset with himself for sleeping in. Finished with gulping down breakfast, he'd pulled on his gear, and without a moment's delay, hustled to the storage garage. A short time later, while guiding the Polaris along the highway trail, he wondered if he was too late to join the search. Most likely all he'd find was a parking lot packed with vacant vehicles.

As he approached the trailhead, the teenager was greeted by more than a dozen empty trucks and trailers strung out along the highway shoulder. More were stationed in the small unplowed parking area. But unlike the day before, a black sheriff's Blazer sat idling at the top of the hill with its rear windows fogged over, making it difficult to see inside. Seth pulled alongside the stubby wagon, switched off the engine, and walked to the passenger door.

A woman sat behind the wheel—a paperback in one hand, a coffee cup in the other. Removing his helmet, Seth gave a quick knock on the window. After a moment of inside activity, the door popped open. "Good morning," the deputy said in a pleasant tone. "They told me you might be coming by this way. You're the Springwood kid, correct? Come in and have a seat."

"Yeah, I'm Seth, Seth Springwood," he answered, slipping inside and closing the door. "I'm the one who dropped Travis off to go camping. I was told it was okay to come up and help with the search."

"Right. That's what they told me, too," the woman said. "Except you're a little late. Everyone headed into the woods over an hour ago. That government fellow did leave a message for you, though."

"What is it? Am I supposed to go back home?"

"No. I'm to tell you that you can use your snowmobile, but only to ride up and down the main trail. That's all. Once you reach the lake, you're to turn around and head back here. You're to check in with me every hour or so."

"That's all I'm allowed to do?" Seth protested, realizing too late his tone of voice made him sound like a spoiled, whiny kid.

"I'm afraid so. Hey, at least you get to ride out in the woods. My assignment is to sit here monitoring the radio. Pretty boring, huh?"

Seth sat silent for a moment, watching melting flakes snaking down the windshield glass. "Can you tell me what the others are doing? Do you know where they are?"

"A few men are going to snowshoe around Mystery Lake. They'll be checking the shoreline for any signs of your friend. Most everyone agreed that, with the weight of the new snow, the ice is much too dangerous to travel on. The rest of Search and Rescue are going to explore other trails. From what those two skiers said, your friend was taking a different route home."

"But that's not true!" Seth exclaimed. "Travis was suppose to meet me here. He wouldn't have changed the plan."

The deputy went quiet, weighing her next words. "We discussed that this morning. The others think it's quite possible your friend did just that. If Travis isn't in the lake, and let's hope that's not the case, he may have decided to take a different way out. Once he hiked to the snowmobile trail, he knew you'd run into him on your way here to pick him up. Makes sense, don't you think?"

Seth shook his head in disagreement. "No, it doesn't. After all our troubles last fall, Travis wouldn't have changed the plan. He knows better than to do that."

Again the deputy was quiet. The police scanner squawked, intruding on the silence. They both listened as another squad called in a vehicle-off-the-road report. When the radio static ended, the deputy returned her attention to Seth. "I gotta admit, I do tend to agree with your theory."

"You do?" Seth asked, making eye contact with the woman.

She returned his gaze and smiled. "Yup. So why are you wasting time sitting here? Climb back on that fancy snowmobile and go find your friend. The day isn't getting any younger."

* * *

Time continued to tick away as Travis toiled frantically on the repair. The task seemed so simple, but every step took longer than planned.

He'd cut four boughs about the thickness of a big man's finger. From these he stripped off smaller branches and needles. Some of the needles he placed into the pot. If he was able to make a fix and head out, he'd need every ounce of reserve his body could muster.

With boughs bare, Travis was ready for the next step. The poacher had stomped both sides of each shoe. A spruce limb would have to be bent and bound to each of the splintered supports. The teen dropped down onto the plank and went to work.

Holding a snowshoe between his legs, he aligned a limb to the outside frame and began the wrapping process. The idea was to tie off in one direction—slowly forcing the limb to bend and form alongside the broken support. Once both sides were bound tight, he would bind the ends together—making one solid unit.

At least that was the plan. But there was a flaw to the strategy. Squeezing the limb to the broken frame forced the support to straighten, causing the webbing to sag like a wet towel. After a half hour of cold hands and stiff fingers, Travis threw the shoe in the snow. He pushed himself up, stood staring at the fire, and began talking to himself. "There has to be some way to make it work. What am I missing? Okay, okay, okay. Settle down. Warm your hands. Have a sip of tea and think about it. You can do this."

After exercising in place to get his blood moving, and sipping a bit of brew, Travis studied the useless snowshoe. Suddenly, like the sun coming out from behind a cloud, the solution came to him. "Jeez! That's it! That's gotta work," he yelled, pushing himself upright.

With renewed enthusiasm, Travis limped to the end of the windfall. He returned to the fire carrying four short, stout branches. When the light bulb had switched on, the teen realized he had to first bind cross pieces to the outside skeleton. Once they were secured, the frames would be held firmly in place. Bending and curving the outer boughs shouldn't have any effect on the inside webbing.

As with all new ideas, the project was more easily imagined than completed. Stopping only to feed the fire, and sip an occasional taste of tea, Travis worked without stopping. An hour later he stood, slipped his good leg into the harness, and took a test step. The shoe was heavy and clumsy. But it didn't sink. The webbing supported his weight.

"One down! One to go!"

* * *

Seth was becoming bored. This was his fifth trip to the lake. Except for waving a greeting to a couple of men returning to the parking area, he hadn't seen anything but trees and snow. He'd reported to the deputy just a few minutes earlier. Nothing of interest had been broadcast over the radio.

"Too bad we can't change jobs," she'd lamented. "At least you get to see a change of scenery. All I've been looking at is a wet windshield."

Approaching a sharp bend in the trail, Seth let up on the throttle. As the machine swung into the curve, a dark flicker off in the woods caught his eye. By the time the snowmobile came to a halt, whatever it was had disappeared.

The teenager sat with the engine idling. Nothing moved, nothing revealed itself. Must have imagined it, he decided, squeezing the gas control. Leaving behind a plume of vapor, he steered around the next turn.

* * *

Fatigue and a falling temperature slowed Travis as he worked with the second snowshoe. With an angry sky overhead, and a useless watch on his wrist, he had no idea of the time. Maybe I don't want to know, he reflected. It might freak me out—probably just a few hours of light left.

His reasoning was accurate. By the time both snow-shoes were ready to march, not much of the day remained. Working in cold, snowy conditions, every task had nibbled at the day. The frigid air and icy mate-rials made fingers thick and clumsy. More and more often as the day waned, Travis found himself kneeling by the fire, warming his hands. The fire often needed feeding—using more precious daylight.

Yet, despite the delays, repairs were completed. Before stowing his gear onto the packframe, Travis took a test hike. No longer did his boots plunge to the forest floor. The snowshoes kept his feet near the top, and though difficult, made walking possible. Now he'd have to hope his knee was up to the task. Today would no doubt be his only opportunity to escape. By tomorrow he might be too weak.

He secured everything but the tent onto the packframe. Because he would be trudging along on snowshoes, he chose to carry his load. He decided the shelter, now covered in snow, would be troublesome and time-consuming to dig out and pack away. And Travis reckoned it was one less thing to weigh him down. Besides, he wouldn't be needing a tent. Once underway, he didn't plan on stopping until he reached help.

Taking one last look to make sure he had everything, the teenager began what would be his final trek. He took a compass reading, picked a large tree in the distance, and began plodding forward.

It didn't take long to realize, even with snowshoes, that hiking in deep, powdery snow was extremely difficult—especially with only one good leg. With so many storm-damaged trees tossed here and there, walking a straight line was impossible. Fifteen minutes into the journey, and already warmed from the effort, Travis stopped to check his progress. His target tree still lay far ahead. Turning to stare at the back trail proved discouraging.

The snowshoe imprints twisted and turned through the tangle of brush as if made by an inebriated blind man. He could still see smoke billowing up from the fire, blending into a metallic sky. His spirits sagged. "Oh, man," he moaned, waddling ahead. "It's gonna have to just be one step at a time, one step at a time."

Finally reaching the first target, Travis stopped to catch his breath. He began searching for the map. It wasn't in his pockets and it wasn't in the pack. When had he used it last? In the tent? Yes—he thought he'd be studying the map again and hadn't tucked it away.

Now what? Leave the gear here on the windfall—hike back and retrieve it? That would use more precious daylight. Could he plot a course without a map? Possibly. He'd need to have confidence in the compass. As long as he walked south and west, sooner or later he should reach the highway. Grinding teeth and clenching fists, he made the decision. Trust the magnetic needle. He'd studied the chart and could picture most of its features. He'd finish the trek without it.

Travis took a compass bearing, and after a quick swig from the water bottle, started laboring toward the next goal. If he was going to make it home, he didn't have time to dwell on things forgotten. He had to look ahead.

Chapter Seventeen

C H A P T E R   S E V E N T E E N

Dusk was approaching—the already murky light was fading fast. In twos and threes, search team members motored their snowmobiles into the parking lot. Tired and hungry, they gathered together, waiting to hear results of the day's efforts.

The news was not good. Not a single clue had been found. They had no more information now than when they'd started. The only nugget of hope was that the snow appeared to be tapering off. If the latest weather forecast held true, an air search could be started at first light.

Though no one said it, most were thinking an air search would be fruitless. Too much time had passed. Too much snow had fallen. If, by some strange twist of fate, Travis was still alive, another day might be too late. Odds were, with the overnight temperature falling far below zero, even a well-fed, experienced camper would find this night to be a test of endurance.

Seth lingered off to the side—listening, thinking, frowning. For almost eight hours he had patrolled the trail. Except for the mysterious glimpse of something dark and shadowy, he hadn't seen a thing to raise his optimism. Studying the faces of the rescue people, he realized there was little hope left.

Somewhere, out in the coming darkness, the body of his best friend might lay cold and still. Although they were different in many ways, Travis and he were like brothers. They had grown up together. Whether working, playing, or just hanging out, what one didn't think of, the other usually did.

Seth had similar feelings at the end of October. He'd found the courage to share a few of his private thoughts at the memorial service held for Travis. During the autumn ordeal, Seth had seen a side of Travis he hadn't known existed. When Seth had become helpless with a broken ankle, it was Travis who had taken charge. Trav had kept the two of them alive in some the nastiest autumn weather Mother Nature could brew. And even though everyone had given Travis up for dead, Seth had held on to a ray of hope.

Did he dare to think the same thing could happen twice? That somehow his buddy could survive the harsh elements a second time? What were the odds? Not good. Almost zero. Seeing the frowns etching the faces of the search team confirmed this thought. It would take a miracle, a major miracle, for his friend to survive. There was little else Seth could do but head for home. At least he'd tried.

With a heart as heavy as stone, the troubled teenager trudged to the snowmobile. Little fuel was left in the tank. He would have just enough gas to make it back to the resort.

* * *

Travis was drained. The injured knee throbbed and protested every grueling step. Walking in snowshoes was not like hiking in boots. Legs had to be spread wide. Each step required extra effort as the foot had to be lifted up and over the snowy surface.

By his reckoning, it was late afternoon. Travis forced a thin, chapped-lipped smile as he added: the middle of the afternoon—in the middle of winter—in the middle of the woods—in the middle of a snow storm.

As quickly as he grinned, he scowled. And I'm about at the end of my rope.

A long, fat windfall a few yards ahead offered itself as a rest stop. The tired teen plodded to the tree, cleared the trunk of steeped snow, and sat. He wasn't making much headway. Imagining the map, he pictured how he had planned on reaching the blacktop. It's no good, he thought. It's too far. I'm not going to make it.

He mulled over his options. There were only two choices. He could stop now, build a signal fire, and hope the sky would lose the overcast. Or he could change course and try to intercept the hiking trail while there was still a bit of daylight left.

Why had he thought he had to get to the highway? So many things had happened the past few days he'd forgotten why that plan stuck in his head. Was it because of the poachers? Maybe. He hadn't wanted to meet up with those outlaws ever again.

That shouldn't matter now, he decided. They'd be long gone. The best chance might be to aim for the hiking trail. The trail should be closer than the road. Maybe, just maybe, somebody is still searching. Maybe, just maybe, someone would find him. He stood, took a new bearing, and plodded forward.

Most of Travis' trudging had been uphill. After another fifteen minute effort, he'd managed to reach the top of a ridge. He stopped to recover his wind and take another compass bearing. If he was going to connect with the hiking path, he'd have to travel more to the south.

He was looking into the forest, seeking his next target tree, when something in the distance caught his attention. Travis knew as soon as he saw the black coat—the yearling. Hobbling on three legs, the pup was coming his way.

Pursing cracked lips, Travis managed a low whistle, stopping the wolf in its tracks. Like a dog responding to its master, the pup doubled its efforts. Travis looked on in awe as the young animal, despite its bad leg, traveled over the snow. When the yearling had closed the distance to a few yards, the animal stopped, sat on its haunches, and looked straight at the astonished youth.

In the same gentle voice he'd used the first day, Travis greeted his wild friend. "Well, Midnight, we meet again. I thought you'd have joined up with your family by now. The way you're able to move about, I'd say you're on the mend. Wish I could say the same."

The young wolf responded with a low whimper. Then it stood, turned in its track, and headed the direction it had just come. Seconds later the pup paused and looked over its shoulder. Travis wasn't sure what it wanted. Was the animal was trying to tell him something? Did the yearling want Travis to follow? If so, where? Why?

The young predator had made its approach from the southeast. If Travis were to snowshoe that direction, wouldn't it take longer to reach the trail? Thinking it over, the teen thought there might be a way to test the wolf. There might be a way to check if his camping companion was actually trying to help.

Instead of following in the yearling's tracks, Travis began tromping toward his next target. It didn't take long for a response. Like a bird dog directing its master, the pup stopped, turned, and bounded back.

Giving Travis a puzzled look, the wolf headed away in the direction it had just come. Again it stopped. Then the animal did something that took the teen by surprise: the yearling yipped. Travis had seen and heard enough. It was obvious the wolf wanted to be followed. Travis turned and waddled after his raven-furred friend.

Deepening shadows stole into the forest as the young man labored to keep pace. The storm's last flurries fluttered in front of a sharp, cutting wind. Stars would be out tonight.

Travis wondered if he would last long enough to see them.

*　*　*

Roger Larsen knelt before the fireplace opening and placed a log on top of hot coals. He jabbed the chunk with a pointed tool, making certain it couldn't topple. After replacing the cinder screen, he stood staring as the log began hissing and spitting, burning on its own.

Across the room, sitting at the large family room table, the remainder of the Larsen family looked on. Seth, his mother, and her friend, Doug Davis, were also present. Seth had returned home to find his mom standing at the door. Earlier she had prepared two large pans of hamburger hotdish. Then she had waited with a butterfly stomach for her son to return. Almost as soon as Seth entered the cottage, he had to go out again. But instead of the snowmobile, he'd hunkered down in the back seat of Doug's big Chevy wagon. The Springwoods were bringing dinner to the Larsens.

Now everyone sat quiet, studying the patterns on the plates—no one sure what to say or how to say it. As hungry as he had been earlier, Seth still hadn't eaten much; neither had anyone else. With supper over, the hotdish pans remained more than half full.

185

Mrs. Larsen appeared as if she hadn't slept a wink in weeks. Dark circles under red-rimmed eyes gave testimony to her worry. After a long awkward pause, Doug Davis broke the lull. "Looks like it's cleared up. I can see a few stars over the lake. There's even a sliver of the new moon just above the far tree line. They'll be able to search from the air tomorrow. If Travis has a fire going, they'll find him soon as the sun comes up."

Roger turned to face the large patio door overlooking the lakeside deck. "The only way Travis could survive is with fire. He's been missing too long to have the energy and reserve to survive the cold tonight. They say we can expect close to twenty below by morning. Even with his full winter gear, that's awfully frigid, especially without having a warm meal in days."

He turned to face the others. "I don't want for us to give up hope. We did that too soon after the autumn storm. But we have to be realistic. What have we had? Two days of steady snow? Three? What would Travis find to eat? Even a seasoned camper would have trouble staying alive and alert this long."

"Roger, you're not losing faith, are you?" Lynn Springwood asked. "We have to remain positive. Travis learned so much about survival in October. And Seth says he's spent the last two months poring over outdoor manuals. We have to believe he can take care of himself."

Mr. Larsen returned his gaze to the patio glass. In the glow created by house lights, the man stared out as bursts of snow swirled and danced across the lake surface. He stood silent, witnessing clouds of white clustering together in drifts along the lake's edge.

The room went quiet for a moment before he responded. "Maybe you're right. We have to hold on to hope. I have to believe he'll find a way to make it out on his own."

After another break, Doug cleared his throat and asked, "What about that government fellow? Has he learned anymore about those two wolf poachers?"

"I have no idea," Roger answered. "He left a message to meet him before sunrise. There's not much anyone can do tonight. Best we all try to get some rest."

On the trip home, Seth gazed out the car window, deep in his own world. Mountains of snow stood guard over the road sides, pushed to new heights by the county plow truck continually patrolling the narrow, curve-filled highway. Seth didn't take much notice. His mind was elsewhere.

Pulling into the resort drive gave proof Rollie had been busy with the pickup. Mounds of white were piled everywhere. On the trip out, Doug had to use four-wheel drive to power up the resort drive. With the path now cleared, he was able to pull the wagon to the cabin's back door. Doug said his goodnights and waited as Seth and his mother entered the cottage. He beeped once, backed up, and drove out.

Inside the cozy cottage they found Sarah at the kitchen table. Before her were hundreds of puzzle pieces waiting their turn to be put into place.

"Any messages?" Mrs. Springwood asked, removing her winter jacket.

"One. Some guy named Higgins. Wanted to talk to Seth. Said he'd call again in the morning," Sarah answered, never lifting her eyes off her work.

"Did he say what it's about?" Seth asked, dropping his boots on the shoe caddie beside the door.

"Nope. Who is he anyway?" Sarah inquired while pushing a piece into place. "Is he part of Search and Rescue? Never heard of him."

"Yeah, you could say that," Seth replied, keeping his promise not to reveal the man's identity, not even to his sister. "Probably wants to know if I saw anything today. But since I didn't, don't have anything to report."

Crossing the open dining area, Seth stopped in front of the large picture window overlooking the lakefront. Through frost-covered glass he could just see the shoreline. The teen turned his eyes skyward. Thousands of stars twinkled in a background of black velvet. On the horizon, looking like a stage prop, a paper-thin slice of moon hung suspended over the silhouetted shoreline. So, he thought, the clouds have gone. Air patrols could begin doing their thing at first light.

Seth stepped sideways to the window's edge and studied the large, old-fashioned thermometer nailed to the sash. The red column was hovering slightly below zero. He frowned. Tomorrow morning might be too late. With a gusting wind, and the mercury falling, even the hardiest of souls would be hard-pressed to make the night. Search and Rescue should be out looking right now, he reasoned. Travis would have a fire burning. Flames would be so much easier to see in the dark.

The teenager said his goodnights and headed to his bedroom. After closing the door, he opened the top drawer of his dresser. Inside was a seldom-used antique alarm clock. Wound and set, he placed the timepiece under his pillow, and then crawled between the sheets, clothes and all.

* * *

Every second step was torment—the knee complaining each effort. Other muscles and nerves were joining the chorus. Travis was using up the very last of his reserves.

He'd been slowly shuffling after the yearling. The animal would hurry ahead until it was nearly out of sight. About the time Travis thought he'd been abandoned, there would be the wolf, resting on its haunches, watching him wallowing after in the snow.

More than a half-dozen times they'd played the strange game of tag. When Travis came close, the wolf would move on. Only this time was different. This time the pup stayed put. It wasn't until the boy was quite near did he discover the reason why.

In the fading light of late afternoon, Travis stopped to take in the scene. A depression had been formed in the snow. Animal tracks were everywhere. Here and there, the white linen had been stained with blotches of dark red. In the center, covered by a thin layer of new powder, were the remains of what once had been a very large deer.

Tall, widespread antlers were attached to the skull. Travis could easily picture what a magnificent creature it had been when alive. Now all that remained were a few scattered bones, curved remnants of the ribcage, and the head with its trophy-sized hat rack.

Standing in place, gawking, Travis felt despair settle deeper into the pit of his stomach. "Is this what the game of hide and seek is all about? I appreciate the thought, but you and your buddies didn't leave much for me. What were you thinking? That I could chew on a bone?"

As if to answer, the pup turned and limped to the antlered head. Opening its jaws wide, the wolf clamped down on the deer's snout. Like a dog playing with a very big stick, the pup began to shake the skull. The antlers were too large, the animal too small. After a moment or two, the yearling released its bite and stared at the boy.

"What? You want brain food? You think I can crack that open? I'd need an ax and I don't happen to have one in my pocket. Besides, I've wasted enough time on this wild goose, or I should say, deer chase."

As spoken words formed puffs of white, Travis felt a wave of nausea, and at the same instant, became dizzy. He had no choice but to plunk down before he fainted. With a couple of unsteady steps, he moved forward into the depression and collapsed.

He lay on his side, the packframe harness biting his shoulders, snowshoes holding his feet off the ground. The prone position helped; blood pressure returned— clearing his head.

With his brain working again, Travis tried to make a final plan. His muscles and bones had been starved and mis-used. They couldn't endure much more abuse. And snowshoeing, he had quickly learned, was far more work than he imagined. Hiking in them was like trudging up a mountain slope wearing heavily-weighted boots.

The wolf had come close. It was sitting only a few feet away. Even in his exhausted state, Travis couldn't help but marvel at the intelligence he saw in the animal's eyes. Wolves, he had learned long ago from his father, were one of Mother Nature's craftiest creatures. They lived in family groups and looked after each other.

Travis pictured the three wolves that had visited the campsite. They must have killed the deer and then led the pup to the meal. Too bad I hadn't arrived here a day earlier, he thought. There may have been a few scraps of meat left on the bones.

Instead, except for some pieces of hide scattered about, the only thing intact was the skull. Did brain have any food value? Travis wasn't sure he really wanted to know. Did he have the time and energy needed to crack the skull? He had the stubby ice chisel. Maybe it would only take a few whacks to get the job done. And a few minutes work would keep him warm.

With the wolf studying his every move, Travis straddled the antlers, aimed the chisel at an eye opening, and thrust the tool with all his strength. The sharp blade hit bone and stopped as if striking stone. The second and third attempts fared no better.

On the fourth thrust the chisel splintered a piece of skull near the eye socket. Travis stood, breathing hard from the labor, and examined the result. Disappointment. His efforts had only taken out a small chip.

Why was he doing this? He didn't want to eat brain, anyway. Looking up, he realized he was losing the daylight. If he was going to save himself, he had to make an immediate decision. Make fire, crawl into the sleeping bag, hope to survive the night. Or keep snowshoeing in the direction of the trail, and keep his fingers crossed someone would find him.

"Sorry, Midnight," Travis muttered, turning to the yearling. "Gotta get going. Can't stay here. But I'll tell you what. I'll give it a few more whacks and you can chew on it later."

The teen made several half-hearted jabs with the chisel, opening the eye socket a bit wider. "There, that's the best I can do. You're on your own."

Bundled in his parka, packframe on his back, he took a compass reading. Dusk was turning the corner to real night and he had difficulty seeing the needle. Satisfied he had the correct course, Travis tucked the compass away, zipped the jacket, and drew a deep breath.

He exhaled softly, then strained his ears to hear any sounds of a search. Nothing—no engine noise—no people noise. Except for the occasional rattling of a tree limb, the silence was intense.

After a dozen painfully slow steps, Travis stopped to take a look over his shoulder. With its ebony fur outlined against the white background, he saw the wolf gnawing away at the skull.

"Couldn't wait for me to leave, huh?" Travis scolded. "Well, good luck, hope you find something delicious in there to eat." With a shrug of his weary shoulders, the boy resumed his trek.

Snow stopped falling shortly after dark. Travis first noticed the change when he halted to take a compass heading. Unlike the last reading, he had little trouble seeing the needle. For some reason the forest seemed a mite brighter. Turning eyes skyward, he was surprised to see stars. Through an opening in the forest canopy, pinpricks of light twinkled down.

Good news, bad news, Travis thought, knowing what clear skies meant. A cloudless sky after a snow event usually ushered in a cold spell, and this far north, that meant well below zero.

Travis hadn't trudged far when the accident took place. It happened as he was climbing over a large blowdown. The sound of splintering wood reached his hat and hood-covered ears. Startled, he wasn't sure what had created the noise.

His next step gave up the answer. As Travis stepped away from the windfall, the webbed shoe on his strong leg twisted, plunging his boot into several feet of snow. The teenager waved his arms wildly, trying to keep his balance, but it was too little, too late.

Almost without warning, he found himself face down in cold powder. There was no doubt to what had just happened. One of the repair boughs had snapped, making the snowshoe about as useful as a flat tire on a freeway.

But what Travis wouldn't know was that the bough had splintered into a dagger-like point. And when he staggered, the sharp end sliced through the tip of his rubber bottomed boot, opening a door to snow and cold.

This isn't happening. It's all a bad dream. I'll wake up and everything will be fine. Maybe all I have to do is go to sleep. Travis had these thoughts because after days of cold, hunger, and frustration, his brain was beginning to wind down. Winter fantasies can strike the fittest and now it was happening to him.

It wasn't because he was freezing. The walking had warmed him. Cold would come later. There had just been too many days of too little food and not enough rest. He had worked his mind and body beyond its limits and was now paying the price—he was losing it. The young outdoorsman no longer had the ability to make wise choices: good decisions that would mean the difference between life and death.

And besides, it felt so fine to rest. All he wanted to do was close his eyes, fall asleep, leave his troubles behind. But first he had to turn over. For falling face first, icy tongues of snow were licking the edge of the mask. Adding to the discomfort was the packframe. The aluminum tubing was biting into his back.

Struggling to his knees, Travis slipped the packframe off. It felt wonderful without the load on his shoulders. Every nerve, muscle, and fiber in his body was numb with fatigue. Now to just curl up and let sleep make his problems disappear.

Chapter Eighteen

C H A P T E R   E I G H T E E N

Seth slowly opened the shed the door, careful not to make a sound. He had been successful sneaking out of the house. He didn't want to spoil things now.

Seth had been certain everyone in the house would wake when the alarm under his pillow had rung. Shutting off the ringer, he had stayed motionless, listening, hoping his mother hadn't heard a thing.

He'd crawled out from under the covers fully clothed—long johns, stockings, and all. His next challenge was to get dressed in snowmobile gear. With help from the stove light, he'd bundled into bibs, boots, and parka, and silently slipped outside. Now, with the shed door open, he stood quiet, wondering if he was making a wise choice.

The mercury had continued to plummet. Each breath sent a little smoke signal into the frigid air. Overhead, clouds had cleared, and the sky was filled with glittery stars. On the horizon to his right, northern lights were on full display. Shafts of green, blue, and an occasional red, lifted and fell like a distant Fourth of July celebration. Awed at Mother Nature's polar light show, Seth stood transfixed, and for a moment forgot why he was there.

It suddenly occurred to Seth that the wind had stopped. The air was bitter cold, but calm. He would have to motor away cat-like so as not to wake the Kanes. His best bet would be to start the engine in the shed, give the machine just enough gas to pull outside, quickly close the door, and go straight to the beach. If he was really going to do this, he didn't have much choice. Tugging the snowmobile down the slope would be impossible, as the snow was far too deep.

Everything went as he hoped. The engine started on the second pull. Finding traction on the concrete floor, the machine jumped into the open. Once the door was shut, Seth was able to coast down the slope using very little power.

With only an occasional throttle burst to stay on course, the teen motored along the edge of the lake, heading toward the boat landing. Because it was two–thirty in the morning, there would be little or no car traffic on the Gunflint Trail. He would ride to the trailhead using the shoulder of the road. He could go faster along the highway than he could by weaving through the much narrower tree-lined trail.

Seth had never snowmobiled so far, so fast. Only once did he release the throttle to slow around a sharp curve in the road. And he had been correct about traffic. There hadn't been any—he was out on his own.

Reaching the turn-off for the parking area, Seth let off the gas and slowed to a crawl. Now that he was here, he needed a strategy. Unless Travis had somehow reached the path since dark, riding up and down the trail would be a waste of time.

Seth firmly believed—if his friend hadn't fallen into the lake and drowned—that Travis would have stuck to the original plan. He would have camped somewhere near this route. Why Search and Rescue had spent so much time looking elsewhere made no sense.

The youth squeezed the throttle, pointed the machine over the hill, and entered the woods. He knew what he had to do. He'd ride the machine nonstop to Mystery Lake. Once there, he'd kill the engine and bellow like a bull moose. He was hoping the clear, calm air would carry the sound of his voice far into the forest. If Travis heard the yells, he'd be sure to holler in return. And if there was no reply, Seth would motor a few hundred yards and repeat the process— over and over.

Scarcely an inch of new snow covered tracks made the previous day. Despite having a packed path, Seth had to go easy. The trail was narrow and filled with twists and turns. He didn't want to over-drive the headlight. Crashing into a tree wasn't part of his scheme.

After having raced at more than fifty miles per hour along the highway, the trail trip seemed to take forever. The teenager was so intent at following the headlight, he missed the turn-off to the lake. It was only after he passed the landing, and came to a fallen tree partially blocking the path, that Seth realized the mistake.

The trail had narrowed and getting the heavy machine pointed in the opposite direction was work. The teen had to climb off, and in short bursts of effort, lift the rear end around. Despite the temperature, the work left him warm and out of breath. He flipped up the fogged over visor, plunked on the seat, and waited for his lungs to catch up.

Upon discovering his mistake, Seth had switched off the engine. As his breathing slowed, he was aware of being surrounded by silence. If it hadn't been for an occasional ticking coming from the cooling engine, he'd have thought he'd gone deaf.

At first the quiet was eerie and Seth felt a twinge of fear. But after a while, his eyes adjusted to the dark and the world took on a new look. What had at first been shadows now had shape. Every tree and every bush was covered in a thick white coat. The scene reminded Seth of a Christmas card, with himself seated in the center.

Suddenly, and very close by, an ear-splitting crack jolted the boy from his thoughts. Terrified, thinking he was the target of some crazy midnight poacher, the youth dove face first from the snowmobile.

He curled alongside the sled, shaking like a leaf, waiting for the second shot. All was quiet. For several long minutes he cowered, scared out of his wits, trying to understand what had just happened.

Except for the pounding of his heart, the intake of air into his lungs, and the pulsing of blood surging past his eardrums, everything was still. Far in the distance came another cracking boom and he began to relax. At once, he remembered this sound—the pop and crack of tree sap freezing on the first sub-zero night of the season. He had heard the same thing other winters. There was nothing to be scared of—he could safely go back to the search.

Moments later, Seth eased the snowmobile down the landing, parked at the lake's edge, and killed the engine. He'd driven slowly without using the headlight. The bright beam destroyed his night vision. With the world mantled in white, Seth discovered he could actually see better without having the light on.

Behind him, over the forest, a sliver of moon had climbed high enough for his shadow to be faintly outlined on the snow-covered terrain. Above and beyond the distant shoreline, the northern lights were in the final act of the evening's performance. The color display had been downsized to a few bursts of white and pale yellows.

Seth studied the multitude of stars overhead until he found the Big and Little Dippers. Using the handle of the smaller dipper as a guide, he located Polaris, or North Star. Like most who grow up near woods and water, Seth took comfort in knowing what direction was which.

He was ready. With a lung full of air, he cupped his hands to his mouth and bellowed at the top of his lungs. "Travis! Can you hear me? Travis!"

Nothing. Not even an echo of his voice returned. It was as if his words had been swallowed by some night creature that feasted on sounds.

Twice more he yelled out his friend's name. And twice more the only sound was that of his boots shuffling snow and his mouth gulping in air. It was time to move on up the trail.

Besides becoming discouraged, Seth was growing hoarse. The teenager had stopped so often he'd lost count. More than a dozen times, he thought. More like two dozen. Each time he'd wait expectantly, hoping against hope, that there would be a return message. That hadn't happened.

Seth was nursing the snowmobile over the crest of a hill when he saw the animal. The youth wasn't sure what he was looking at. Whatever it was, it was certainly easy to see. The black coat stood in stark contrast to the ivory backdrop.

Seth instinctively squeezed the brake and shut off the engine. He had expected the animal to turn and bolt, as wild animals do when a human is near. But that hadn't happened. Instead of turning tail, this creature of the night crept closer. And as it did, Seth recognized it for what it was—a wolf. Not a very large wolf, but a wolf nevertheless.

This was a strange event. Black-furred wolves were rare. That one was out alone in the middle of the night was spooky. That the animal didn't high-tail it away when he approached was downright bizarre. Seth had several quick thoughts, none good. Was the predator sick? Did it have rabies or some other disease? Did it see him as an easy meal?

Just as Seth was about to restart the engine, the wolf did something even more unpredictable. The wild dog let out several yipping barks, turned, and headed back the way it had come. The wolf stopped after three or four hobbling steps, looked over its shoulder, and barked out another yelp.

Seth sat fascinated. This was more than weird. It was almost if the creature was trying to communicate. Impossible. It's an animal—a normally shy, seldom seen, wild animal.

As if running out of patience, the yearling gave one more sharp bark and limped farther into the forest. Even in the shadowy darkness, Seth could see that the animal was injured. Healthy wolves bound or leap through snow. This one moved as if it had a broken leg.

What to do? Should he start the snowmobile, and keep with his plan? Or should he stay put, see if the mysterious critter returned? Seth was about to yank on the starter handle. Suddenly, the stillness was broken by a spine-tingling wail. The haunting howl started as a low moaning whimper, rose in pitch and volume, and then faded off to a pitiful whine.

Seth had heard wolves before. Many times. But never like this. And never so near—so close—so loud. The primitive cry set his heart racing, and despite his warm winter gear, ran shivers up and down his backbone.

What did this all mean? Why would this young wolf broadcast its presence? Was it to tell friends and family about a foolish boy traipsing around the forest—an easy meal? No, that didn't seem right. Wolves never attack healthy humans. They learned eons ago to fear people— to run away—to stay hidden. This whole black and white scene was becoming more and more of a riddle.

Seth sat quiet, staring off into the shadows, pondering the situation. Then, there it was again. The wolf had returned. Its black fur outlined clear and defined against the white forest floor. Just as it had done before, the animal yelped, turned, and limped away.

He had seen enough. Nervous or not, Seth wanted to get to the bottom of this mysterious behavior. Releasing a pair of aluminum snowshoes from the carrier rack, he stepped into the bindings and secured them to his boots.

If only he had a weapon. The shovel might work. Rollie had long ago clipped a small folding spade below the rear seat. "Just in case," the cautious resort owner had said. "Just in case you ever have to dig your way out."

With the tool open and ready in one hand, a flashlight in the other, the teen stepped off the trail. The snow- shoes were small emergency models and the first few strides were awkward. Unlike the shoes he used on the day he'd found the wolf hide, these dipped deeper into the quilt. But after a dozen or so clumsy steps, Seth got the hang of it and felt sure he'd stay upright. With a last look at the snowmobile, he waddled after the animal.

Seth connected with the wolf's path forty yards into the trek. Even with meager moonlight, the tracks were easy to spot. The animal had come and gone the same way several times. Following the trail was far easier than he had expected.

He hadn't gone far when he saw the wolf in the shad- ows ahead. The raven-furred predator was standing in front of a rather large windfall—its nose pointing at the ground. Another decision: Does a fourteen-year-old boy really want to approach a crazy-acting animal in the middle of the night?

With that alarming thought, the teen stopped mid-step. Then he saw something else. A few feet from the wolf, resting on the snow, Seth thought he recognized the outlined shape of a packframe—rolled up sleeping bag and all. For a moment the boy's heart seem to stop, only to begin beating wildly in his throat. Could it be? Or were shadows playing tricks?

Terrified at what he might find, Seth stood transfixed—heart pounding. Finally he couldn't stand the suspense. He had to know. He had to look. But first, to be safe, the wolf needed to be frightened away. With a big breath, Seth began bellowing. "Eeeeeyah! Scram! Get!"

Startled by the sudden outburst, the animal jumped, spun around, and limped to the end of the windfall. It stopped there for a moment, looked over its shoulder, and with its head hanging low, loped away on three legs.

* * *

Sunrise was still a far off promise when the phone pleaded to be answered. Half asleep, Mr. Larsen managed to pick up on the third ring. "Hello, this is Roger," the groggy man mumbled into the receiver. "What?" Roger was now wide awake. "Where do you think he went?" he asked. There was a pause, and then: "I can't believe Seth would do that. Just take off in the middle of the night without telling anyone. You say he took the snowmobile? Let me think about it for a minute."

There was a momentary lull as Roger processed what he'd been told.

"No, don't call anyone else just yet. I'll get dressed and take a run up the highway in the wagon. If I see a fresh snowmobile track we'll know what he's up to. And Lynn: if I learn anything, I'll come home and give you a call. Don't get stressed out. I'm sure he knew enough to wear his warmest outfit."

Roger listened another moment before ending the conversation. "Okay then, stay put. I'll get back to you in an hour or so."

Mrs. Larsen had switched on the reading light over the bed. She, too, was now wide awake. As her husband set the handset down, she had to ask. "Don't tell me. Seth went out on his own looking for Trav, didn't he? My God, Roger! What's with these boys? Do they have a death wish? It must be ten below out there."

"Honey, Seth will be fine. I'm sure he's dressed for the weather. He must be feeling guilty for not tagging along with Travis in the first place. You know how he keeps things to himself."

"But still, Roger, that's no excuse for taking off in the middle of the night. Lynn must be going crazy with worry."

"Let's remember he's out looking for our son. And that's just where I should be. Now that the snow has ended, Seth no doubt decided there'd be a better chance to spot a fire or hear a yell. And you know what? He's absolutely right. I need to go out and join him."

"No! No! Don't let this be!" Seth cried out. Forest shadows hadn't played tricks. There was no doubting that the pack-rig resting in the snow belonged to his buddy. Seth saw something worse—much worse. Alongside the blowdown, curled in a sleeping position and showing no sign of life, was his very best friend.

"Oh, my God! Don't let him be dead! Don't let him be dead!"

For a moment, Seth was too stunned to do anything but stand petrified in place, staring at Travis' rigid form. This was what he had feared. They had looked too little, too late, and mostly in the wrong places. Drawing a breath, Seth tried to calm himself. He had to be certain. He had to check for a pulse, for a heartbeat.

Quickly removing his snowshoes, Seth tromped to his childhood companion. Even in the meager light, he could see that his buddy had been bundled in warm winter clothing. Covered with a ski mask, his friend's face was scrunched against the sleeves of the winter jacket. Seth removed a glove, and then with trembling fingers, reached down. He slid his hand between Travis' mask and folded arms.

A surge of hope welled up, warmed him, pushed aside some of the fear. Seth had expected the touch to be cold—cold and hard as a fish left to die on the ice. Not so. His nervous fingers felt a hint of warmth—a hint of life.

Forgetting everything else, the young man sprang into action. The first thing Seth did was roll Travis over—not an easy thing, but Seth never noticed. He yanked up the mask and placed his cheek next to Travis' nose, hoping to feel a breath. Yes! Slow, faint; too meek to hear, but a whisper of warm air.

What now? Seth wracked his brain. Muttering out loud, he gave himself directions: "Gotta get him awake. Gotta get him awake. I gotta get him awake."

Grabbing Travis by the shoulders, Seth muscled his pal into a sitting position. "Come on, Trav! Wake up! Wake Up! Ya gotta wake up!" He repeated over and over while shaking Travis like a giant rag doll. No response—no reaction.

Seth released a shoulder and began slapping Travis on the cheek. Gently at first, then with more force, hoping for some sign of life. Frustrated and frightened, he was about to quit, about to try something different, when Travis suddenly shuddered. "What? Stop it! Quit hitting me!" Travis gasped in a tiny child's voice. "I'm tired. Let me sleep. Just let me sleep."

Overjoyed, Seth continued to slap his friend's face. "Come on, buddy! Wake up. It's time to go home. Then if you want, you can sleep for a week."

* * *

The Suburban sped down the blacktop; its headlights cutting a wide swath in the clean, calm air. Caught in the bright beam, and looking like precious gemstones, millions of snow crystals blinked back from snow-banks lining the roadside.

Roger was convinced he knew where Seth was heading. He'd spotted the snowmobile track crossing the road-way at the end of Poplar Lake. Following the track was easy. It was imprinted in the road's snow covered shoulder. The teenager was headed for the trailhead. No doubt to have one last look before the air search began.

Moments later the vehicle slowed and swung into the parking area. The small unplowed lot looked much as it did when Roger had left the previous evening: cold and empty.

Engaging four-wheel drive, Roger powered the vehicle through a maze of truck and snowmobile ruts. For a moment the tires lost traction and he thought the vehicle was stuck. Then, just as suddenly, the wheels caught and the wagon shot forward, not stopping until the headlights lit up the trail entrance.

Sure enough, imprinted in the last thin layer of snow was a single snowmobile track. So Seth had gone out exploring on his own. But what to do about it? Other than Mrs. Springwood being upset, the boy wasn't in any real danger. Roger checked his watch. In a few hours the woods would be full of people. Seth would have lots of company.

There was little that he could do. He could wait and see if Seth returned, but that might not be until dawn. Probably best to go home. Call Lynn. Console and calm her. Share what he'd learned. Roger was putting the car in reverse when a glint of light far off in the timber caught his eye. The flash was brief, and had he been looking elsewhere, he would have missed it completely.

Roger stared into the forest's shadows, wondering if he'd caught a reflection of his own headlamps. No.

There it was again, brighter, closer. The snowmobile headlight. Seth had to be coming up the trail.

The light winked through the trees more and more often as the snowmobile made its way along the forest path. Roger sat nervously awaiting the teen's return. What had the youth hoped to find in the middle of the night, anyway? This trail had been repeatedly patrolled without a clue of Trav's whereabouts.

The beacon grew brighter. Then the snowmobile was out in the open. For a moment all Mr. Larsen could do was sit and stare. Silhouetted against the picture postcard background, he could see two people. The front passenger was hunched over. The rear rider was standing, arms extended, guiding the machine up the hill into the parking lot.

For an instant Roger thought Seth must have talked his sister, Sarah, into going along on this mid-winter's night ride. But then, as the snowmobile cut across the car's headlights, the man was grabbing for the door handle. He'd gotten a glimpse of the front passenger's parka. Roger had purchased the garment as gift. Bright yellow, a special mountain climbing model, designed for the worst of winter weather. And because of the close call after the autumn storm, Roger hadn't waited to play Santa. He'd given it to Travis at Thanksgiving.

With a burst of power, the snowmobile was up the slope and alongside the vehicle. Tears of joy blurring his vision, Roger Larsen swept his boy into arms as if he were a small child.

"Thank God! Thank God!" Roger kept repeating over and over, laying his cheek against his son's cold face. "Thank God!"

* * *

Roger stood staring through the lobby window. Below him, at the base of the hill, the town of Grand Marais was beginning to wake up. Plumes of dusky white spiraled from chimneys, climbing quickly toward the clean sky. Far off to the east, the first rays of an unseen sun fanned over the horizon with a blush of color. After days of reflecting only charcoal gray, Lake Superior joined in the show. Its surface captured reds and yellows, blended them together, and mirrored back a golden sheen.

The man saw none of this. He was in a world of his own. Roger felt like pinching himself to be certain this was real. Travis was safe. Cold, exhausted, maybe even a bit frostbitten, but okay. This was going to be a wonderful day, a glorious day—a day the family would never forget.

After placing his son in the car, Roger had driven directly to the hospital. The boy hadn't said much during the trip to town. All Travis mumbled was that he just wanted to sleep. That was to be expected. After all Travis had been through, he'd need time to recuperate.

Roger waited until his boy had been wheeled into the emergency room before calling Linda. She'd picked up on the first ring, giddy with joy. The Springwoods had already phoned. After transferring Travis from the snowmobile, Seth had raced for home. Within minutes of his barging through the cottage door the call had been made. So now, between his wife's sobs of joy, Roger repeated what he knew about Travis' condition.

"Yes, he's going to be all right. He's tired and hungry, but he's okay. The doctor's examining him right now." Roger held the phone away from his ear. His wife was speaking so fast, so loud, he was sure everyone in the building could hear.

"I don't know. Possibly a finger tip or two," Roger replied to a question. "It's too early yet to tell about his feet. They don't want to warm him up too fast. His body's been stressed enough." Again the man held the phone inches away.

"Yes, honey. He was wearing his insulated boots. They're rated for fifty below. His feet should be fine. But to be truthful, I didn't take time to check."

The conversation went on like that for another five minutes. Roger finally ended it. "Look, why don't you call Lynn and tell her that you and Beth will pick her and Seth up in a few minutes. It'll be a little while before they're through here. You might as well drive in daylight."

There was another pause as Mrs. Larsen bubbled on about the news. "You're right. I don't know how we'll ever be able to thank him. See you in an hour or so, okay?"

Roger put down the phone and walked to the window with its panoramic view of the big lake. He was busy thinking. Who else should know? For sure, the sheriff deputies. He needed to make that call right away. The rescue party and aircraft pilots were probably already on their way out.

The special agent, Higgins, should be notified. Roger had another thought. Maybe the whole search team should keep the news under wraps for a day or two. If Seth was correct in what he'd heard, maybe that Higgins fellow could think of a way to charge the poachers with more than stealing a wolf's fur coat.

Within the hour a small crowd clustered in the lobby. No word of Travis' condition had yet been reported. Seth was in the center of the room, sprawled in one of the overstuffed chairs. Sitting across from him on a large floral print sofa, Linda Larsen waited expectantly for Seth to speak. The rest of the group, including her husband, stood quietly behind, equally interested in what they were about to hear.

It was Roger who spoke first. "Seth, what you did tonight was risky, but we thank you for doing it. Even if a search plane managed to spot Travis this morning, it would have probably been too late."

"Sure sounds like it," a deputy added. "But what we want to hear is how you knew where to look? The search team had been up and down that hiking trail dozens of times. You included. What made you go back there in the middle of the night?"

Seth cleared his throat. He never liked being the center of attention. At least telling so many people at once meant he wouldn't have to repeat the story over and over. "Well, I guess it was the change in the weather. Once the snow stopped, and the sky cleared, I figured if Trav had a fire burning, it would be easier to spot in the dark."

"That makes sense," Roger praised, "but why the trail? Like the deputy said, we'd scoured that area."

Seth stopped studying the carpet and looked up. "Cause that's where Trav said he'd be. I knew after all our troubles last fall, he wouldn't have changed the plan. Everyone else wanted to believe those poachers. I knew they were fibbing. And I bet they had something to do with Trav's close call."

With a nod of his head, Agent Higgins agreed. "Could be. We'll talk about that later. Right now you're keeping us all in suspense. How'd ya do it? How'd ya manage to do what the rest of us couldn't?"

"I had help," Seth said. "I don't know if you're gonna believe what I'm about to tell you. It's really strange, more like weird. A wolf, a jet-black yearling wolf, is the real hero."

The group stood with eyes wide and mouths open as Seth recalled the night's events. No one interrupted—

no one as much as coughed. When he was through speaking, the lobby went quiet.

For a long while not a word was uttered. Then Roger asked the first of many questions to come. "You said you left the trail and used snowshoes to hike into the woods. After you found Travis, how did you manage to get him on the snowmobile?"

"Yeah. That was a bit of a problem. I knew I couldn't carry him. Snow's too deep. Even with those small snowshoes, I'd have sunk to my knees. What I ended up doing was tramping back to the snowmobile. Since I had already made a path, I was able to drive right into the woods."

Seth made eye contact with Rollie Kane. "You aren't going to be real happy. Kinda dinged the hood in a few places."

"Nonsense!" Rollie laughed. "Seth! You know me better than that."

"Yeah, just teasing, Rollie. Besides, it's nothing the two of us can't fix."

"So, how did you get Travis on the Polaris?" Roger asked eager to hear all of it.

"Well, once I got back to where I found him, I had to lift the rear of the snowmobile around. Travis was sorta awake, but pretty much out of it. I had to muscle him around, too."

The sound of footsteps cut the story short. From down the corridor the doctor was approaching, a wide smile lighting his face. "Morning Linda, Roger," the slender, white-clad man announced, waving a clipboard at the rest of the group. "And a good morning at that," he beamed, unable to keep his findings a secret.

"Okay, first the good news. We've been able to bring Travis' body temperature up to near normal. All his vital signs are good. For what he's been through, I'd have to say they're great. I think that by the end of the day, with a little rest and some fluids, he can go home."

"Really? That sounds terrific. But you said good news first. What's the bad news?" Roger asked, an arm tight around his wife's shoulder.

Still smiling, the doctor answered. "There is a chance that Travis has a bit of frostbite."

Mrs. Larsen took a gulp of air and gasped. "Where? How bad?"

She worked at this hospital. She'd seen the results of frostbite. It killed living tissue. Fingers and toes turn black and, because hope for healing is lost, they are surgically removed.

"Linda, I said a bit of frostbite. Even with those high-tech arctic boots, a little toe got nipped by Jack Frost. You know what to look for. Keep an eye on it for the next few days."

The doctor paused to glance down at the clipboard. "He does have another problem. One knee is sore and swollen. My guess is badly strained ligaments. We have him in x-ray right now, but I really don't expect to see any bone damage. And at his age, he'll mend fast. You'll just have to keep him inside for a while."

"When can we see him?" Linda asked, rising from the sofa.

With a nod of his head and a smile, the doctor answered. "In a few minutes. They should be about done taking pictures."

Later, most of the early morning visitors departed to go about their regular routines. Roger and Linda were keeping a bedside vigil, patiently waiting for Travis to talk about his brush with death. Neither one wanted to pressure him. They knew when he was ready to share, he would.

Travis was sitting up, sucking a thick shake through a fat straw. A knock on the open door was followed by a uniformed deputy entering the room. Agent Higgins was trailing close behind.

"Good afternoon," the deputy grinned, stepping over to the bed. After brief introductions, and beaming down at Travis, he continued, "You think your boy is up to having a little bedside chat?"

"I think so," Linda replied. "But you'll have to ask Trav. He thinks the doctor should release him. Says he doesn't know what all the fuss is about."

"That right, Travis? You ready to go out and play in the snow?" the deputy asked.

The youth stopped sipping long enough to answer. "Not really. Don't know that I'll ever want to go out on my own again."

"Hmm…I guess I can understand why you'd feel that way. But I think in time you'll get over it," Higgins offered.

"I don't know about that. I never told anyone, but the reason I went camping in the first place was to get over my fear of being alone. Didn't work out that way though, did it?"

"Oh, Trav," his father sighed. "The two ordeals you've been through the last few months would have tested the best. It's perfectly okay to be afraid. That's normal. What you do about it is the real test. And Travis, you pass with flying colors. Don't you agree, gentlemen?"

"Absolutely," the deputy nodded. "Courage comes from inside. And you seem to have plenty. I don't know many people who could have endured the hazards you've faced, what with the knee and the way the weather turned foul."

"Right," Higgins added. "Travis, being afraid when you're threatened is as natural as knowing the sun will rise each day. All heroes experience what you're feeling. What separates the heroes from the rest is being able to think your way through to a solution. And most importantly, not to panic—to use brain power—to keep one's wits. And I gotta tell you, young man, you seem to be a champ in that department."

"I sure don't feel like a hero. I was scared stiff the whole time. 'Specially when that creep tied me to a tree."

Linda let out a loud gasp, bent over, and placed her face next to her son's. "Oh, Travis, you must've been out of your mind with fright. I had no idea."

Roger clamped one of his ham-sized hands on his son's shoulder and gave a loving squeeze. "Neither did I. Travis, whether you agree or not, you are our hero. You're more than that. You're a hero and a survivor. We're very proud of you."

Travis set the malt container on the bedside table, swallowed, and then exclaimed, "Really? What about Seth? He's the brave one."

"Yep, he's a hero, too. But you managed to keep yourself alive until he found you. That took some real grit," Roger smiled, rubbing his hand over his son's shaggy head of hair.

"I think you were both brave," Linda added. "There's room in my heart for two champions."

Travis broke into a grin, then looked at the two men standing near the bed. "I suppose you want to know what really happened back at Mystery Lake, huh?"

And so the tale was told. Mostly the adults listened. When Travis reported how he was tied to a tree, Linda cried out and started mumbling. "How could they? How could they? How could anybody be that cruel?"

Travis waited patiently for his mother to calm before continuing. "I think it was mostly the tall dude's idea. By the way, that guy sure does stink. He must live in a cabin without running water. Anyway, from what I saw and heard, he seemed to be the boss. The other fellow, the short fat one, I think he was afraid of his partner."

When the story was complete, no one knew what to say. After hearing what Travis had endured, all were amazed he was here to talk about it.

"Well, fellows," Roger began, looking at the lawmen. "You said Seth finding the wolf skin and rifle wasn't enough evidence—that the bag could have been left by anyone. I'd say you have plenty of proof now."

"Maybe for killing the wolf," the deputy answered. "Providing, of course, you let Travis testify. However, proving kidnapping or attempted murder might be a bit more difficult. It's your son's word against theirs."

Agent Higgins scratched a whiskery chin in thought. "We need some kind of plan. We have to get that pair to admit to their foul play."

"That's not likely to happen," the deputy replied. "They'll continue to cough up a bunch of bull feathers. No way will they ever admit to anything."

Roger came up with a plan. "Higgins, that bag Seth found. Anyone besides those of us here know about it?"

"Just Rollie Kane. Why? You have an idea?"

"In a minute. Those poachers. They're not the brightest pair of porch lights on the block. After the New Year, when Trail visitors have left for the cities, and locals go back to work, don't you think those two will return for their treasure?"

"Ah," the deputy chuckled, seeing where Roger was heading. "Yup. They won't want their special package to go unclaimed. They're bound to come back for it."

Roger looked at his son and smiled. "Okay, I have a plan. It means Travis will be spending a little more time outdoors. But I think it might work. It just might work."

Chapter Twenty

CHAPTER TWENTY

"Trump!" Seth announced, placing his cards on the small folding table. "Let's see. According to my calculations that makes two million, three hundred thousand you owe me."

"Yeah, well good luck trying to collect," Travis shot back.

It was two days after New Year's. Outside, the sun was just about to call it a day. Tucked far back in the forest, the olive-green Army tent was already in deep shadows. From a cot in one corner of the canvas dwelling came the soft sounds of sleep. Agent Higgins was catching some shut-eye. He would be the one to monitor the radio during the long, black evening hours.

"Tell ya what," Travis bartered, "before it gets too dark, deal one more time, double or nothing."

The two pals, along with Higgins, were camped for the second night deep in the pine grove. Others had set up the large walled tent not far from where Seth had found the wolf skin. Entry to the area had been from far down the Gunflint Trail. Special care had been taken not to leave tracks anywhere near the poachers' stash site.

The biggest hurdle had been getting Mrs. Larsen's approval. After all the arguments had been gone over, time and time again, she finally relented. The tent had a heater. There would be cots to sleep on. One of the deputies, a mountain of a man who hiked for a hobby, would carry Travis to the tent. Seth could keep Travis company. There would be two-way radios, warm sleeping bags, plenty of food and snacks, and most important, Agent Higgins promised not to let Travis out of his sight.

Several miles away, along the Gunflint, deputies were posted—except they didn't look like lawmen. In one direction they had parked a logging truck on the road shoulder, marking the area with reflector warnings to slow traffic. Dressed in old work clothes, the deputy was to keep a close watch for anyone matching the poachers' general descriptions.

Farther up the Gunflint, well past the pine plantation, several deputies sat on snowmobiles, one with the hood up as if it had mechanical problems. All had state of the art electronics—two-way radios that couldn't be heard on a police scanner. All they had to do now was hope and wait.

Inside the cozy shelter, the boys continued to banter. "Double or nothing? Do I look like a fool?" Seth quipped, shuffling the cards. "On second thought, don't answer that."

"Yup, you do. Just make sure I get a good hand. I think you've been dealing your cards from the bottom of the deck."

"Yeah, right. Like I had such talent. Speaking of hands, how are your fingers feeling?"

"Fingers feel fine. It's my little toe that hurts." Travis continued in a whisper: "Didn't want to say anything. Mom would have made me stay home."

Seth finished shuffling and began distributing cards. "How bad? Maybe it's not such a good idea for you to be here. Maybe your mom's right. Maybe you should have stayed home. Frostbite's nothing to fool with."

"And miss the chance to trap that foul-breathed fool who left me to die? No way!" Travis snapped, rearranging his cards. "And by the way, thanks. I think you just dealt me some winners."

The boys finished the last game, and true to his prediction, Travis had a winning hand. Seth was securing the deck with a rubber band when the radio suddenly crackled. "Unit One to Base Camp. Over."

Higgins was instantly wide awake. He keyed his radio to acknowledge the call. "Base here. What do you have?"

"Prepare for visitors. Trav's camping cronies just passed the checkpoint. Older model Ford pickup, green in color. White camper top with a broken back window. The red-bearded dude was driving. My hunch is he's going to drop off his buddy, then keep going up the Gunflint. Probably plans to kill some time before retrieving his pal on the return trip."

"Roger that, Unit One. Unit Two, did you copy?"

After a short pause, a new voice squawked through the small speaker. "That's affirmative. Want that I should flag him down? Stall him a bit with a request for assistance? Over."

Higgins thought for a moment before replying. "If it works out, fine. Just don't tip our hand. Another squad can pull the pickup over later. With all the snow, and the Gunflint being a dead end, there's really no place for him to go. Over."

"Roger that, Base. I'll play it by ear. Good luck on your end. Over."

Higgins slid the radio into its belt holster. Standing tall in the darkening shelter, he made his announcement. "Showtime! Travis, are you certain you're up to this? We don't have to do it this way."

The youth was quick to answer. "Yeah, I am. Besides, how else can you make the case? You said yourself that it was only my word against the two of them."

"Okay, then. Let's bundle you up and get you out there. If that tall fellow's wearing snowshoes, it'll only take him a few minutes to hike in."

Travis was already dressed in bibs. After first pulling on the yellow parka, Higgins helped Travis slip into the shoulder straps of the packframe.

The backpack had been Seth's contribution. Returning home from the hospital visit that first day, Seth had spent that afternoon recovering Travis' camping gear. It hadn't been difficult. He was easily able to follow his own tracks to the rescue site.

Seth had even taken time to mark the area with red surveyor's tape. In the spring, before leaves opened, Seth figured that he and his buddy could have a fun hike looking for the tent. After all it had been through, the little shelter deserved a better fate than to be just left to the elements.

Higgins held the flap open as Travis limped out. The boy's snowshoes were standing upright in the snow. Slender pine-pruned branches had been lashed to the frames, disguising the fact the shoes had been expertly repaired.

Higgins leaned in close and whispered. "And remember to stay hidden until he finds the package. When he does, make your move, but don't get too close. The microphone is super sensitive. It can easily pick up a man's voice from twenty or thirty feet. And don't worry. I'll be watching you the whole time. If that sorry excuse makes any threatening move, I'll be on him faster than a used car salesman on a tire kicker."

Buckling Travis into the snowshoe bindings, Higgins reached into the rear flap of the backpack. "Soon as I turn on the recorder, you're good to go," Higgins said softly.

"Let's go over it one more time. Try to startle him, make him think he's seeing a ghost. Once he starts babbling, guide the conversation along. First talk about the wolf and then how he kidnapped you. I promise, if you can get it on tape, he'll be watching the rest of his sunsets through steel bars."

Higgins pulled his hand from the pack, gave Travis' head a rub, and mouthed, "You're on the air. Good luck."

"Do my best," Travis replied quietly. Without another word, the lanky teen began plodding over the snow. For the present, his aches and pains were forgotten. This was payback time and Travis was planning to collect.

Unit One's hunch had been right on the mark. The battered pickup slowed, then stopped, as it approached the stand of evergreens. The taller of the pair, still outfitted in white, popped out of the vehicle. He went quickly to the rear of the truck, reached through the missing window, and retrieved a beat-up pair of snowshoes.

Just as fast, he returned to the passenger side door. "Twenty minutes," he yelled through the glass. "And if there's any other traffic, don't even slow down. Go down the Trail a ways, turn around, and try again. I'll stay hidden behind the plow ridge. Got it?"

Coughing out a cloud of blue smoke, the pickup lurched forward and headed down the highway. In several strides the long-legged outlaw climbed over the snow bank. He was quickly out of view from any passing traffic.

He smiled, thinking how easy this had been. All he had to do was retrieve the gun and pelt, climb in the truck, and head for town. Sweet—a piece of cake.

* * *

Travis was crouched behind a giant fallen aspen. He was in open woods, having left the cover of the pine grove to get within yards of where the garbage bag and its contents had been returned. At first that had been the sticky point of the plan. How could the package be replaced without leaving tell-tale tracks?

Seth had come up with the solution. It was his chore to clear the walkways and steps of resort cabins. The winter before had brought nightly dustings—too thick to push with a broom, not heavy enough for the large motorized snow-thrower.

Lying in bed one night, and weary from shoveling and sweeping, the answer came to him. Rollie had a powerful gas-powered leaf machine. Seth tried it and it worked well. For the rest of that winter the teen had given new meaning to the term 'snow-blower.'

Rollie had rummaged around the storage shed until he found a pair of ancient over-sized snowshoes. Higgins had worn the relics while replacing the garbage sack. Once the bag had been hidden, he'd backed away, using the leaf blower to erase all signs he'd been there. Seth's idea worked like a charm. The leaf machine blew up a blizzard of snow. Even in daylight, not a trace of a track remained.

Travis heard the poacher approaching. Dressed in grungy white, the wolf-killer moved like a phantom. Only his beard stood out. Dark and shaggy, the unkempt facial hair bobbed up and down like a plump bird in flight. In the murky light, the balance of the man's body was almost invisible.

When they'd discussed it, the scheme had seemed simple. But now, with his kidnapper so near, Travis wasn't so sure. His breathing had become fast and shallow, and he could feel his heart hammering. Much like a puddle on a warm day, what courage he had left was quickly evaporating. Gulping a breath of air, he slid low against the blowdown and kept telling himself to stay calm. "You can do this. You're not alone."

The teenager took another large breath before lifting his head for a final glance. The coverall clad figure was almost to the tree root mound. Only a few more steps and it would be time for Travis to make his acting debut. Time slowed to crawl. It had to be timed perfectly. The poacher needed to be behind the root mound and out of sight.

As the poacher disappeared from view, Travis rose unsteadily to his feet. The plan was not to approach the man directly. Rather, Travis was to plod past, fifteen or twenty yards away as if lost and exhausted. To avoid suspicion of a trap, Higgins wanted the poacher to discover Travis, not the other way around. The boy was not to even look in the man's direction until the disclosure had been made.

It wasn't hard for Travis to look worn out. His mother had insisted the injured knee be wrapped and braced. Snowshoeing in deep powder with a stiff leg was awkward. No acting skills required. Travis kept his head down—eyes forward. He didn't have to feign surprise when his presence was detected.

The poacher's raspy voice bellowed without warning. "My gawd! I don't believe it! Is that you, kid?"

At first startled, Travis remembered his role. And though the sound of the poacher's voice caused him to quiver, he played his part well. The teenager turned to face the enemy. Even in low light and fifteen yards away, Travis could see a hateful look on the man's whiskered face.

"Mister, I need help. I'm lost and hungry. You gotta help me."

The poacher had already retrieved his treasure. The bag lay cradled in his arms as if it were a bundled baby. With a look of disgust, he let it drop to the snow. "Help you! Why in blazes would I help you? You've caused me too much grief as it is!" the scofflaw roared, taking several long strides toward Travis.

This wasn't happening like they'd planned. Somehow Travis had to direct the conversation. "Do I know you?" he asked innocently, trying to hide his fright.

The reply was almost the jackpot the lawmen wanted. "Know you? What kind of fool question is that? You know darn well who I am. Don't be pulling that memory loss crap on me."

Taking a few more steps, the poacher cut the distance in half. Now he was close enough for Travis to see the anger in the man's eyes. But the creep hadn't really said anything to admit guilt. Travis needed to press on.

"Really? I don't think I've ever seen you before. You live around here?"

Like a fish to a lure, the poacher swallowed the bait. "Kid, until the day you die, I know you ain't gonna forget what I done to you. Stringing you up to that tree and leavin' you for bear bait."

The outlaw had moved even closer. So near, Travis thought he could smell the stink of the man's foul breath. "Oh," Travis said, taking an uneasy step backward. "Would you be the one that shot a wolf back at Mystery Lake? I was beginning to think that was just a bad dream."

The statement, said so innocently, was enough to put the man over the edge. "Bad dream? You know damn well it was no dream. Tonight's gonna be your real nightmare. Who'd a thought you'd still be alive? This time I'm gonna have to finish the job myself."

In a flash, the poacher was on Travis. One minute the jack-o-lantern mouth had been flapping threats. Then in a blur, the man was standing nose to nose. "You got 'bout ten seconds to say your prayers, boy. Better make 'em good."

Travis couldn't decide if the light-headedness came from fear or was caused by the man's putrid breath. What he would later recall was being toppled backward. The poacher had straddled Travis and was about to grab him by the neck. Terrified, Travis tucked his head tight to his chest and closed his eyes. Where was Higgins? Why was this happening?

The next thing Travis heard was a thud and a grunt. Like a sack of sand, the would-be killer collapsed across him, pushing Travis deeper into the soft snow. Confusion mingled with fear as the youth struggled to push the poacher off. The frantic efforts only caused Travis to burrow deeper into the powder. Then, as he was about to thrust with all his might, the weight was gone. He was free. He could breathe.

"Sorry it took so long. Didn't want this creep to see me sneaking up on him," a voice said, adding to Travis' confusion. "I waited 'til the last minute. I really didn't want to have to pull the trigger."

Travis managed to sit up. Next to him, the poacher lay face first in the snow, one hand on the back of his head. That the would-be killer had been whacked on the skull, the teen could understand. It was who had done the whacking that had Travis puzzled. The person holding a shotgun in his arms wasn't Higgins. It was his buddy, Seth.

"Let's tie this guy up before he comes 'round. I'd feel a whole lot better knowing he can't go anywhere," Seth said in his usual calm voice. "Better yet, we can use these handcuffs I took from Higgins."

Without uttering a word, Travis struggled to his feet. This was crazy. Why was Seth here? And where was Higgins? This didn't make any sense.

Seth handed the gun to Travis. "Here, hold this. If he tries anything, fire it into the air. That'll get his attention."

Travis tentatively took the weapon, and then watched in awe as his husky friend yanked back one, and then the other, of the man's arms. Almost as if it was something he did every day, Seth snapped the man's wrists into a pair of shiny steel handcuffs.

Turning to Travis, Seth smiled. "There, that should hold him until the deputies arrive. How ya doing? Did he hurt you?"

Travis finally found his tongue. "What's going on? What are you doing with a gun and cuffs? Where's Higgins? I don't get it."

"Surprised, huh? Me, too. Tell ya about it in a minute. First, let's give a holler everything's okay." Seth turned to face the pine grove. In a huge voice he boomed, "Yo! All clear! Can you hear me?"

From somewhere in the evergreens a voice echoed back. "Roger that. Stay put. Help's on the way."

For a brief moment the woods were hushed. Then their prisoner let out a long low moan. "He's coming around," Seth said. "Guess the deputies won't get the pleasure of dragging him face first through the snow."

Seth started to explain why he, and not Higgins, had been the one to save the day. "Well Trav, seems our federal lawman kept a secret from his boss. Turns out…oh, here he comes now. I'll let you see for yourself."

Travis turned. Through the forest shadows, a human form could be seen shuffling in their direction. Travis didn't understand. Higgins stood tall and walked with long powerful strides, even with snow-shoes on.

The figure drawing near looked nothing like that. Bent at the waist, and using a stick for support, the form was moving with a lack of grace and with the speed of someone ancient in age. Whoever it was stopped and yelled. "Seth? Travis? Everything okay?"

Travis had no trouble recognizing the voice. It definitely belonged to Agent Higgins.

"Yup," Seth replied. "Take your time. I don't think Trav's friend is in any hurry to get up."

With that remark the poacher let out another long groan. There was little doubt that Seth's use of the gun stock would give the man a lasting headache. From the direction of the highway came the whine of snowmo-bile engines. Unit Two had arrived. Headlights bounced and weaved through the trees as the machines followed along the poacher's trail.

In took only moments for two burly riders to reach the scene. Killing the engines, the deputies jumped from the snowmobiles, and wallowed in knee-deep snow to the prisoner. Satisfied the man posed no threat, they turned their attention to the boys.

"You did good," the taller of the two said, taking the shotgun from Travis. "Where's your leader? This wasn't the way it was supposed to go down."

"Right here," a voice replied. Agent Higgins, bent and in obvious pain, trudged up to the group. "I have some explaining to do. Travis, thank God you're not hurt.

You too, Seth. If anything had happened to either of you, I'd never forgive myself."

"Looks like you're the one with a problem," the second deputy observed. "What went wrong?"

"We can talk about that later,' Higgins said, obviously embarrassed. "Travis? Did we get what we need?"

"More than enough, sir. Maybe you should stop the tape. I haven't had a chance."

"Right," Higgins agreed, reaching into Travis' pack. When he removed his hand, he was holding a palm-sized recording device.

The deputies had pulled the prisoner to a sitting position. With the aid of a flashlight, an officer knelt to check the man's pupils. "He looks awake enough to me. What do you think, Jerry?" The deputy asked his partner. "Think this guy's okay to make the hike to the road?"

The officer continued to shine the flashlight on the poacher's face. Finding himself handcuffed, the poacher was beginning to understand what was taking place. He grimaced at the light, revealing the mouthful of missing teeth.

It was Seth's remark that made the group chuckle. "Trav, you're description of this guy was right on. His face does kinda look like a Halloween mask. 'Specially with that toothless grin. Remind me to brush after every meal."

"What, I look like your mother?" Travis quipped. "I don't know about the rest of you, but I'm getting chilly standing here. How 'bout a ride to the road?"

"You got it, young man," the taller deputy replied. "Unhitch those webbed shoes and hop on. By now one of the squads should be parked along the shoulder. You'll be warm in no time."

A little later, the blacktop was alive with flashing lights. Everyone had been ferried from the woods, including an uncooperative captive. The deputies had read the suspect his rights and had placed him in the back of a Blazer. In a few minutes another squad would arrive with his partner. The rotund little man had offered no resistance when pulled over and arrested farther up the Gunflint. Soon both prisoners would be warm and snug, sharing a cell as guests of the county.

Agent Higgins and the two teenagers were warming in the cozy comfort of the Larsens' big wagon. Roger had been waiting anxiously at home. He'd rushed to the scene immediately after receiving the call from the sheriff's office.

No one said a word as they watched the Blazer make a U-turn in the middle of the highway. Finally Roger said, "Higgins, there are a couple of very concerned women waiting for their boys to return. Let's say we go back to the house and hear how it went down over a cup of hot chocolate? Everyone okay with that?"

Hearing no disagreement, Mr. Larsen put the car in gear and headed for home.

Chapter Twenty-One

C H A P T E R   T W E N T Y · O N E

Everyone had gathered in the Larsens' large, open living space. For the first time in nearly a week, the Christmas tree in the corner was alive with colorful lights—reflecting the group's mood. Two happy mothers, Rollie and Katie Kane, Agent Higgins, Sarah and Beth, and even Doug Davis and his little girl, Cindy, were anxiously awaiting the details of the capture. In the large fieldstone fireplace a bright blaze snapped and crackled behind the cinder screen. The room buzzed with joyful conversation as they anticipated Travis joining the group.

Upon arriving home, Travis had gone directly into the bathroom. He needed to look at his frostbitten toe. The teen hadn't been completely honest. The tiny limb pained him far more than he'd led everyone to believe.

After removing his sock, Travis stood with his foot on the edge of the tub. The swollen tip of the tiny toe had turned an angry black. Travis knew what that meant—another trip to the hospital. But that, he decided, could wait until morning. Why spoil the mood tonight?

"Here he comes," Travis' younger sister, Beth, announced in her most grownup voice. "Trav, I saved you a place by the fire. We want to hear the whole story."

"Me too," Travis said, hobbling into the room. "Nobody's told me why it was that Seth had the pleasure of bopping that bugger on the head." Travis grinned at his pal. "I was expecting someone older, someone a lot better-looking."

"Oh, man," Seth snorted. "Looks like you're back to normal. Just remember, we're about even. You took care of me after the autumn storm. The past few days I got to return the favor."

"Enough, already," Linda Larsen admonished, smiling. "We're waiting. Who's going to start?"

Higgins cleared his throat, twisted uncomfortably in his chair, and looked around the room. "Why don't I begin? First off, I need to apologize. Mrs. Larsen, Roger," he said, meeting the elder Larsen's gaze. "About two years ago, while trying to push a pickup out of a ditch, my feet suddenly slipped. The unexpected jolt put my back out of place. For a couple of days after that I could hardly move."

"Sure know 'bout that," Rollie Kane blurted out. "Some weeks my back goes out more than I do." The group all had to laugh despite the interruption.

"Yeah, well, I didn't. This was a new thing for me," Higgins continued. "I was just about to see a doctor when the darn thing slipped into place."

This time it was Travis who broke the narrative. "What's that got to do with tonight?"

Higgins looked at the sandy-haired youth, smiled, and went on. "I'll get to the point in a minute. I never reported the incident to my superiors. I didn't want to be pulled from field duty. I'd probably be assigned to a desk. I love being outdoors. Rather quit than switch to a desk." He hesitated—remembering. "Since the time with the truck, my back's only gone out twice.

Once 'bout a year ago while splitting firewood, and then of all times, tonight."

"So that's why you were walking so slowly," Travis said. "What made it happen tonight?"

"Soon as you left, I started to bend over to fasten my snowshoes. One boot was down into the snow more than the other. I must have twisted as I bent over. Wham, like an ax hit my spinal cord, I was helpless. Whatever caused it, I knew I wasn't going to be any help to you."

"So how did Seth wind up with a shotgun and hand-cuffs?" Travis asked, eager to hear all of it.

Higgins took a sip from the mug he held in one hand, and looked at Seth with a sheepish grin. "Your buddy heard my grunts. Never saw a kid move so fast. One look at me and he was dressed in a flash, ready to fol-low in your tracks. I told him 'no way, too dangerous,' but you know how you kids listen to us grownups."

Higgins went on. "Seth pulled the shotgun—it's only loaded with birdshot by the way—and my extra set of cuffs from the tent. He told me to follow when I could, and then took off. He'll have to tell you what happened after that. I was a little slow getting to the scene."

Seth blushed as all eyes turned his way. As usual, he didn't like being the focus of so much attention, but tonight he didn't have a choice. In a soft voice, the nor-mally shy youth explained how he had followed Travis' tracks to the edge of the pine grove. Already knowing where the bag was placed, he decided to move closer to the road and stay hidden. Once the poacher passed by, he'd simply trailed the man back to the stash site.

The scary part had been to know when to make his move. "Sorry, Trav," Seth said. "I didn't want the creep to hear me coming up behind him. That's why I waited so long before butting him with the gun stock. It was that or firing the gun in the air to scare him off."

Travis shot Seth a teasing look of disgust. "Thanks a lot, pal. If you called it any closer, it might have been too late. I think the creep was planning on breaking my neck."

"Stop!" Linda Larsen interrupted. "I've heard enough. Mothers aren't supposed to hear these things. The important thing is you're both safe."

"How 'bout we all have a second cup of cocoa?" Roger beamed. "Then some of us would like to hear the whole story from top to bottom. Just one more time, starting with the very first day."

The fire had turned to coals by the time Travis finished. Though tired and ready for sleep, both boys did their best to answer questions.

Sarah, Beth, and little Cindy had listened, spellbound. That a wolf, a yearling at that, had kept Travis company—and in the end, was responsible for his rescue—was something out fiction. Those things weren't suppose to happen in real life.

"Dad, why do you think the pup stayed with Trav? Wouldn't it have wanted to join the pack?" Beth asked.

"Sweetie, I've thought long and hard about that. I'm not certain. Best answer I can give you is that when it was hurting, Travis became a substitute parent. More people should act like wolves. I don't mean the killing part. They only kill prey to survive. I mean the caring part. Family groups usually look after each other."

Roger deliberated, his eyes fixed on the coals in the fireplace, before going on. "You know, they're incredible creatures. That's why I do my research. They're extremely intelligent. Wolves usually pair for life and teach their young good manners. I think Trav's Midnight was just returning a favor."

"What's going to happen to the wolf now?" Sarah asked. "Is he going to die?"

"From what Travis and Seth have said, I think he'll be okay," Higgins volunteered. "Wild critters heal fast. They can't afford to take time off for a hospital stay. What do you think, Rog? You're the wolf expert."

Roger took a moment to ponder the question. "If the pack accepts him back, he'll be fine. And I think they will. Why else did they share the deer kill? It sounds like one of his legs is already healed. My best guess, since the bullet came from a small caliber rifle, the other one will mend, too."

Higgins gave a grunt as he stood to leave. "Let's continue this discussion tomorrow. What I need now is a firm mattress. My back can use some mending. Let's all meet at the Poplar Place in the morning. Say nine or so. I'm buying breakfast. We can do the paperwork later."

"All of us?" Rollie laughed. "Sure you can afford it on a government salary?"

"Mr. Kane, it'll be my pleasure, even if I have to take out a loan."

Seth let out a big yawn. "Mom? Can we go now? I need to get a good night's sleep. I see a tall stack of pancakes in my future. I'll need all the rest I can get."

Tired as he was, Travis didn't get much sleep that night. He found it hard to believe one little toe could cause so much agony. But, in the morning, and despite his discomfort, he kept mum until everyone had filled up on bacon, eggs, and buttermilk pancakes. How often, he figured, would a federal agent buy him a meal?

Travis didn't mention his problem until the family was all seated in the car, ready to head to town for some shopping. At the clinic the doctor insisted the lawmen's paperwork would have to wait. The tip of the little toe had to come off—immediately. The chance of infection—or worse—was too much to risk.

From that time forward, whenever Travis would shower, bathe, or go barefoot, he'd have a tiny reminder of his cold winter quest.

about the author

Minnesota native Ron Gamer has held a passion
for woods and waters since early childhood days.
Now retired after thirty-four years of teaching in the
Robbinsdale School District, he continues to be active
in the outdoors. When not out fishing, bow hunting,
or piloting small aircraft around the state, Ron can be
found at his computer—creating realistic adventure
he hopes will be enjoyed by readers of all ages. *Winter
Chance* is the second title in a proposed 'Travis and
Seth' trilogy.